SUSAN GATES

VIRIDIAN

QUICKSILVER

CHAPTER 1

It was a hot, sunny afternoon in July when the Verdans stopped at the American Diner.

Jay Rainbird, fourteen years old, was outside, flipping burgers on a barbecue. Behind him, the Diner flashed in the midday sun. Jay's dad had towed the retro American trailer to this weedy wasteland beside the motorway. Then he'd put up a sign: 'OPEN. Best Burgers in England.'

'Green freaks,' murmured Jay's dad, as the Verdans' car pulled up.

Jay had seen them, driving up and down the motorway, and on TV of course. The plant virus that had spread to humans had been the main news for months now. Every time you turned on the TV, you saw doctors and scientists discussing the virus, or Verdans talking about what it was like to have chlorophyll skin.

And they all seemed to agree. They'd found the secret to a happy life.

One said, 'I'm saving the world.'

Another said, 'My acne's totally gone!'

There just didn't seem to be a downside to being a Verdan.

'I'm going to put up a sign,' said Dad. '"We don't serve green freaks here".'

'You can't do that, Dad,' said Jay. 'That's prejudice. And anyway, we need the business.'

Jay desperately wanted the Diner to do well. In the three months they'd been open, Dad had been focused, not restless at all. But Jay couldn't relax. He half expected to wake up one morning to find Dad and his motorbike gone and a note that read: *Sorry son, I just couldn't hack it. Got to move on.*

'Don't be rude to 'em, Dad,' begged Jay. 'They're everywhere now.'

'Doesn't mean I have to *like* them.'

'But they're saving the planet – turning carbon dioxide into oxygen when they breathe. And they never cause any trouble.'

Dad couldn't argue with that. When people caught the plant virus, they became contented and serene. They said, 'Life's so simple now.' They stopped fretting about all the things they'd wanted before – more money, the latest mobile.

Dad saw the pleading in Jay's eyes. 'All right,' he relented. 'I'll serve them. But they'd better not get too close.'

'You won't catch the virus, Dad,' said Jay. 'Not unless your blood gets mixed with theirs. And that's not going to happen, is it? Just be careful.'

Like they'd been careful for months now, if they were around plants, making sure they didn't have a bleeding wound that came in contact with live plant sap. Dad had bought some big bottles of strong antiseptic. He swore that would stop them getting the virus, if they poured it straightaway on an infected wound. Even though they told you on TV that antiseptic was no use at all.

'I still don't like those Verdan creeps,' muttered Dad. 'They make my skin crawl.'

At first, most people had felt like Dad. There'd been mass panic when, months ago, a few fruit pickers in Spain had been infected by plant sap through cuts and scratches. The patients were quarantined, while scientists frantically searched for a cure. Then the virus began to spread. People all over the world caught it: gardeners, hikers, kids building dens in the woods.

But instead of growing, the panic began to die down. Because all the patients insisted they weren't sick. In fact, they felt great! All their human health problems vanished, even heart disease or cancer. 'It's like we're brand new,' they said. 'Like we've been born again.'

Jay couldn't keep up with events. But then, he hadn't been paying that much attention. He'd been deliberately blocking out the world beyond the Diner. He didn't want anything to upset his dreams, of him and Dad being together, a family again, happy ever after.

The Verdans got out of their car. There were four of them, two adults, a boy aged about sixteen, and a younger girl. They came walking towards the Diner.

Dad strolled over to meet them. He was running his hands up and down his wiry, tattooed arms. He only did that when he was nervous.

'Hi!' Dad greeted his new customers, remembering to switch on a smile.

Jay let out the breath he'd been holding. You never knew how Dad would react. Gran said that Dad was unreliable. That he'd never grown up.

'Want to sit in the shade?' Dad asked the Verdans.

Dad had set out chairs and tables outside the Diner in a sunny space, well away from nettles and brambles that might infect you with the virus. Some of the tables had big green umbrellas shading them.

'Oh, no shade please,' said the Verdan woman, shuddering. 'We love the sun. We hate the dark.'

'OK,' shrugged Dad. 'Whatever you want.'

From his burger station Jay couldn't stop staring. *Dad's right, they are creepy*, he thought, then immediately felt ashamed.

The plant virus had turned their skin green, reptilian. Their hair was green, even their fingernails. But it was their green eyes that freaked Jay out the most and made them look like aliens.

The others sat, but the girl skipped into some tall nettles, sliding between them, blending in, so you couldn't see which were the plants and which was her.

Jay automatically said, 'Hey, be careful.' But of course

she didn't have to be careful around plants: she'd already got the virus. She was a plant hybrid herself now. The nettles wouldn't even sting her.

The girl came out again and sat down in a chair, beside her mum. But she didn't make any eye contact with her parents. She was humming a little song, her green face calm but strangely detached.

So far, so Verdan. But the boy surprised Jay. He wasn't gentle, like Verdans were supposed to be. He was a Verdan with attitude. He sprawled in his chair, his long legs stuck out. He ran a hand through his straggly, green hair and scowled, like any bored, resentful teenager.

The mum seemed friendly. She was asking Jay's dad about the trailer.

'They call them Silver Bullets in America,' Dad was telling her. 'Me and my son Jay, we live in the back part. I stripped out the front, made it into a Diner.' Dad couldn't keep the pride out of his voice.

'It's a cool trailer,' agreed the Verdan dad.

'I towed it up here from the South Coast,' said Dad. 'Jay's gran lives over there in Franklin.' He jerked his head towards the nearby town.

'Oh, we live there too,' said the woman. 'We're almost home. But we were so dried out. We couldn't wait for a drink.'

The Verdans might be strange, but they seemed harmless enough, Jay thought. After a while, you probably wouldn't even notice the green.

Dad asked, 'So what can I get you? Coffee? Coke? How about a burger?'

The burgers were sizzling on the grill. Jay flipped them one last time. He was sure they'd be tempted by Rainbirds' burgers, with cheese and all the trimmings.

But the Verdan mum said, 'Just fresh water please. Rain water if you've got it. Otherwise, tap water will have to do.'

She smiled at Dad. She had pale green teeth. When he'd first seen Verdans on TV, those green teeth had freaked Jay out. They were like the teeth of the undead in horror films. But now, Jay found, they didn't even make him shudder.

'Just rain water?' Dad was asking Mrs Verdan. 'Nothing to eat?'

The boy yawned again, unfurling a tongue like a thick, green furry leaf. 'All we need is sunlight, CO_2 and water,' he said, in a slow, bored voice, as if he'd explained this a hundred times before. 'We don't eat the crap you do.'

Jay watched Dad's face anxiously. Dad didn't like being talked to as if he was stupid. Especially not by some smart-arsed, green-skinned kid.

And then the boy did something that made Jay gasp. He kicked out at a chunk of loose tarmac, which sailed towards the Silver Bullet.

Jay thought, *Oh no*! If it hit, made a scratch on that dazzling metal, Dad would have a fit. Luckily, it fell short of the trailer. But Jay saw the muscles in Dad's face tense with anger.

'What's your name, son?' said Dad.

'Viridian,' said the boy, defiantly. 'It's a shade of green. My sister is Sage. That's a shade of green too, in case you didn't know that.'

'I did know that,' Dad told him, his eyes glinting dangerously.

Jay waited, every nerve screaming. *Don't lose it, Dad*, he was thinking. *Stay cool*. But those muscles in Dad's face were twitching.

Then Dad shot Jay a look that seemed to say, *Viridian! What kind of name is that?* And to Jay's relief, he realized Dad's face was twitching with laughter.

'You all have to change your names to something to do with plants?' asked Dad. 'Like if I became Verdan, I could be called Sap, or Sucker?'

Viridian didn't smile. 'We don't all change our names,' he said. 'But me and Sage did, to show how loyal we are to the Verdan cause.'

Dad nodded, hardly bothering to hide his grin. 'Well, that's nice, Viridian. Want a Coke, Viridian?' he added, rolling the name off his tongue, very slowly, syllable by syllable.

Viridian's green eyes blazed with fury. He opened his mouth to speak. But the Verdan dad chipped in, as if he was scared of what his son might say.

'Unfortunately, fizzy drinks are like poison to Verdans,' he explained. 'It's the bubbles, you see. Too much CO_2 has a terrible effect…'

'OK,' said Dad. 'Four glasses of rain water, coming up. You want ice and lemon with that?'

'No lemon,' said Viridian, sternly. 'We don't eat plants. We respect the green world.'

His shoulders shaking with silent laughter, Dad went to fill glasses from the water butt behind the Diner. As he passed Jay, he rolled his eyes.

Viridian got up and strode around, walking off his anger. He came over to Jay behind the barbecue. His alien eyes rippled with eerie, green lights. His skin looked supple and smooth as water lily leaves.

Jay forced himself to look straight into those hostile eyes. He noticed, for the first time, that Viridian's skin was a much darker green than the rest of his family, and wondered why that was.

'I'm sorry you got the virus,' Jay said, trying to be nice. 'That was really bad luck, your whole family getting it.'

'Luck?' said Viridian, scornfully. 'We *chose* to be Verdans. We got injected, all four of us.'

'You got infected, like, *deliberately*? You mean, this injection actually *gave* you the virus?'

'*D'oh*, yeah,' said Viridian. 'Don't you watch the news? Humans are queuing up to become Verdans. At least, everyone is who isn't stupid. Soon, there'll be more of us than there are of you.'

Jay stared at him in disbelief. 'Come on! That's never going to happen, is it?'

Viridian didn't even bother to answer. Instead he said, in a voice dark with menace, 'So you'd better tell your dad, it's time he took us seriously. Soon *you'll* be the freaks, not us.'

'Hey, wait a minute,' said Jay, forgetting he'd meant to be nice. 'Who are you calling a freak? Have you looked at yourself in the mirror lately?'

Viridian fixed Jay with a stare so intense and chilling that Jay felt himself shrivelling inside.

'You tell your dad,' said Viridian, 'to give me some respect. And you tell him to remember my name. Because he's going to hear it again. I can guarantee that.'

CHAPTER 2

Dad was behind the Silver Bullet.

There was a small brick building here, which held the generator and a deep freeze, and a rusty old metal shipping container, big enough to walk inside, that they used to store soft drinks and catering packs of margarine, tomato sauce, mustard and cooking oil. Beside the generator building was a water butt.

Wonder if they mind green scum and dead flies? wondered Dad as he scooped out the first glassful of rain water.

Suddenly the Verdan girl skipped into view.

'Hi,' said Dad awkwardly. He had no idea how to talk to a Verdan kid.

But the kid ignored him anyway. She came skipping over to the water butt, leaned over and stuck her head, right up to the neck, in the water.

Her green hair floated on the surface like river weed. Millions of tiny oxygen bubbles clung onto her green skin and fizzed to the water surface like champagne bubbles.

Dad stared, astonished. She still didn't come up. Then he

started to worry: *Can she breathe down there?* She didn't seem to be in any distress. But what if she was drowning?

He couldn't take the chance. He grabbed the back of her T-shirt, hauled her out, and dumped her on the ground.

She twisted round. 'I was thirsty,' she said. 'I didn't drink enough yet. What did you pull me up for?'

She stared at him accusingly through her river weed hair.

Oh no, thought Dad, panicking. What if she started howling and her parents came running?

'Look, don't cry, I'll give you a drink,' he said. 'Just don't cry, OK?'

* * *

Over by the barbecue, as Viridian and Jay glared at each other, a terrible high-pitched scream rose above the growl of motorway traffic. Viridian's green neck slowly twisted round.

'It's Sage,' he said.

He went strolling towards the Silver Bullet in long, loping strides, with Jay running to keep up.

Viridian's mum and dad watched, their faces showing no particular concern, as their daughter raced in a shrieking frenzy through the tall grass. Her eyes were staring and wild, her skinny limbs jerking, her head wobbling. She had a giant, empty pop bottle clasped in her hand.

'Who gave her the fizzy drink?' said Viridian. 'She's got a CO_2 rush.'

Sage flung down the bottle, went streaking across the tarmac and sprang at the wall on one side of the wasteland. It was high, built of crumbling brick and almost swamped by a creeping mass of dark green, dusty ivy. With manic energy, Sage began scrambling up.

Her mum called out, 'Excuse me, where's my rain water?'

Jay and Viridian arrived at the bottom of the wall together.

'Come down!' yelled Jay. But Sage climbed higher with shocking speed, her skinny body swallowed by the ivy.

'She's nearly at the top,' said Jay. Motorway traffic roared by on the other side of the wall. What if she climbed over and fell? Or ran out into the road?

Jay's heart was thumping wildly. But Viridian's green face looked smooth and unworried.

'What's wrong with you?' Jay yelled. 'It's your sister up there!'

Desperately, Jay plunged into the tumbling jungle of ivy, hauling himself clumsily up, grabbing at leaves. His feet scrabbled for the twisted ivy creepers that suckered themselves to the brick. Whippy stems tugged at his clothes. It was like climbing through a strangling maze.

Viridian appeared beside him, climbing easily. His dark green skin merged with the leaves as if he and the plant were one. Only his pale denim jeans and white T-shirt showed up.

Dust and bits of ivy showered on Jay's head as Viridian

overtook him. Jay clung to the ivy, coughing. *How far am I from the top?* he thought. He looked up to check and through shaking leaves he saw Sage. She was balanced on top of the wall, standing with her eyes closed, her arms outspread, as if she was going to fly.

Just below her, six lanes of motorway traffic thundered by.

An ivy creeper ripped off the brick and lashed his bare arm. Jay swore at the stinging pain, praying he hadn't been scratched. He reached blindly upwards, one hand groping through the creepers for a more secure handhold. The ivy seemed to be fighting him all the way.

Viridian was already at the top.

He grabbed his sister's ankle. Sage swayed, bent forward as if she was going to dive head first into the traffic. Then Jay suddenly burst free of the ivy and grasped her other ankle. Together they dragged Sage down off the wall.

Sage clung to the ivy with amazing strength, her green fingers curling round its creepers.

'Let go,' Viridian ordered his sister.

Jay was hanging on grimly too. The ivy felt loose, as if it was going to rip away from the crumbling bricks in one great green sheet and send them hurtling to the ground.

'I can't hang on much longer,' Jay said through clenched teeth.

Viridian bent back Sage's fingers to try and break her grip. Sage howled at the pain but didn't let go.

Viridian shrugged. 'Let's leave her.'

'*What?*' gasped Jay, thinking he hadn't heard right.

'Just leave her!'

Then, as if her energy surge had slumped to zero, Sage let go. It was so sudden, Jay wasn't expecting it. She simply went limp and dropped, crashing through the leaves. Horrified, Jay stared downwards, and saw his dad, at the bottom of the wall with Sage in his arms.

Dad called up, 'I caught her, she's safe.'

Jay watched as Dad put Sage down beside her parents, who barely glanced at their daughter.

'Where's my rain water, please?' demanded Sage's mother. 'My skin is so dry.'

Dad stalked to the Diner. He came back with two glasses of rain water and slammed them down in front of Sage's parents. They poured the drink down their throats.

'Ahh,' said the woman. 'I feel so much better.'

Already her face seemed plumper, juicier. Water, in tiny glistening droplets, began to transpire from the pores in her green skin.

Dad, you kill me, thought Jay. *All the times I need him, he doesn't show. Then he turns up and casually saves some kid from breaking her neck.*

As his tension drained away, Jay felt tired and weak. Following Viridian down through the tangled creepers, he had to concentrate to make sure he didn't fall. When he reached the ground, his legs were wobbly.

Viridian said, 'You cut your arm.'

Jay inspected the long gash. It was shallow but it was bleeding a lot. He felt a wave of panic. Had it been a scratch from a plant?

Viridian was bleeding too, from a cruel-looking cut on his wrist. Jay saw blood oozing out, green as plant sap. He stared at it, repelled and fascinated.

Jay was about to say, 'I never knew your blood was green too.' But he gulped back the words, confused by the strange, intense glow in Viridian's eyes.

Viridian stepped closer. Jay felt suddenly light-headed as he breathed in the oxygen from Viridian's photosynthesizing skin.

'You could be one of us,' Viridian hissed. 'Right now. We can save the planet. You polluters, you're killing it, with all your poison gases and dirty waste.'

Viridian held up his bleeding wrist. Jay watched the green blood trickle down his arm. He looked down at the dark red blood still leaking out of his own wound.

'You want us to mix blood?' said Jay. 'So I get the virus?'

Viridian nodded.

'No way.'

'What are you scared of?' said Viridian. 'Becoming a Cultivar is the biggest adventure ever.'

'Becoming a what? I thought you were a Verdan. I've never heard of Cultivars.'

'You will,' said Viridian. 'We are the future.' He gave Jay

an odd smile, secretive and arrogant. 'You'd make a worthy Cultivar. You did well, back there. But if you want to be a Cultivar, you must be a Verdan first.'

Viridian lunged forward, grabbed Jay's arm, and clamped it against his cut wrist.

Jay struggled and shouted, 'Let me go!' But it was too late. He saw their blood mingle, run in red and green streaks down his arm.

Viridian watched it, fascinated. He whispered, 'I made a new Verdan.'

Jay couldn't speak. His brain felt numb.

'I made you,' Viridian was saying dreamily. 'We're joined together blood to blood...'

Suddenly, Jay woke up to the horror of what had just happened. 'You green freak!' he screamed, tearing his arm away. 'You've given me the virus!'

He started running back towards the Silver Bullet, shouting 'Dad, Dad!'

Dad came rushing out of the Diner. Jay held up his bloody arm. 'Viridian gave me the virus! We both got cut climbing after Sage and he just grabbed my arm...'

'What!' Dad exploded.

He hustled Jay inside the Diner. Shivering, Jay watched him unscrew a bottle of antiseptic. 'It won't work, Dad. Nothing works, they said so on TV...'

Then he yelled out as Dad poured the contents of the bottle over his arm. Jay hopped around the trailer, cursing at the burning pain, then threw himself down on the tiny sofa.

Dad leapt down the trailer steps. 'I'm going to get that green freak,' he shouted back to Jay. 'Teach him a lesson.'

'Dad! Don't!' pleaded Jay. 'Don't go after him! He's different from the others. He's dangerous!'

But Dad had disappeared. Jay sat shivering on the sofa, cradling his arm. He didn't have any faith at all in the antiseptic. The doctors on TV had said, over and over again, that nothing could stop the virus. Once you'd been infected, you saw the first signs really quickly. The skin around the wound bleached grey. Then it turned green. And then the virus would spread to the rest of your body and your brain.

Jay waited, his nerves shrieking. He felt like throwing up. His eyes stayed fixed on the wound. But it didn't change.

Then Dad came back into the trailer. 'They've gone,' he said. 'Just driven off.' He knelt down to look at Jay's arm.

'Dad, I don't think I'm infected,' said Jay, his voice shaky, but with a hint of hope.

'Told you that antiseptic would do the trick,' said Dad. 'That stuff would kill anything.'

They waited some more. Still nothing happened.

'Don't worry,' said Dad finally. 'Panic over. You're not one of them green freaks.'

Jay took in his first, deep breath for what seemed like ages. He let it out in a long, shuddering sigh of relief. 'I was really scared.'

'No need to be scared now,' said Dad.

'I'm not!' Jay protested. He stopped hugging his arm and stood up. He even managed a feeble grin.

'Hey, Dad,' he said, 'you were a hero out there, catching that girl. I bet her parents didn't even say thanks, did they?'

Dad said, 'No, but then, it was my fault she went hyper in the first place. I gave her a bottle of fizzy pop.'

'What? Her dad told us it was poison to Verdans! Why'd you give her that?'

Dad shrugged. 'I didn't think, did I?'

Jay sat in silence for a minute. Then he said, 'Dad, have you ever heard of Cultivars?'

'Culti-whats?' said Dad.

'Cultivars,' said Jay. 'Viridian said he was one, that they're the future. Do you know what he meant?'

'No idea,' said Dad. 'He was some kind of psycho, if you ask me. I've never seen Verdans behave like that.'

'I know,' said Jay, nodding.

'Well, I'm not taking any more chances,' said Dad 'I'm going to put up that sign – "No Green Freaks Served Here".'

'Dad,' protested Jay, wearily.

'All right,' said Dad. '"Sorry, No Verdans Served Here". That polite enough for you? But I *definitely* don't want any more of 'em stopping at my Diner.'

CHAPTER 3

A few weeks later, Jay walked down the slip road carrying the 'DINER OPEN' sign.

A lorry thundered past, making him stagger in its slipstream. But after that, there were big spaces between cars and lorries. There hadn't been much traffic yesterday, or the day before.

He was setting the sign up on the dusty verge when he noticed Dad's other sign, the one warning Verdans not to stop at the Diner. Someone had painted big red childish letters all over it:

POLUTORS LIVE HERE

Jay decided to take the sign back to the Diner. But as he was walking back across the wasteland with it, he heard Dad yelling, 'Jay!'

Jay dumped the sign and started running. 'Where are you?'

'I'm out the back!' came Dad's voice, shaking with anger.

Jay skidded round the back and found Dad staring at the

trailer. The same person had painted graffiti there too, low down on its gleaming aluminium side. This time it said:

POLUTERS MUST DIE

Dad was so choked with fury he could hardly speak. 'Look what they've done. I'm never going to get that off.'

The rusty old shipping container had the same words scrawled all over it. But Dad didn't care about that. All he cared about was the Silver Bullet.

Dad spat out, 'Wait until I get my hands on him!'

'Who?'

'That Viridian kid of course. He must have done it last night. I never heard a thing.'

'Neither did I,' said Jay. He thought about how easily Viridian had snaked through that ivy. He could slither through the thistles and stinging nettles behind the trailer without making a sound.

Jay imagined Viridian, in the dead of night, peering through the windows of the trailer with those spooky green eyes, watching them sleeping.

'There's no proof that it's Viridian,' said Jay, trying to calm himself and Dad down.

Dad was too angry to reason with. 'Whose side are you on?' he snapped. 'Why do you think it's not him?'

Jay said, lamely, 'He'd do better graffiti than that. And he wouldn't spell "polluters" wrong.'

But he didn't dare tell Dad the real reason. Viridian had

said he and Jay shared a bond, blood to blood. And he'd said that Jay was worthy of being a Cultivar. Jay was flattered – and curious.

It's the biggest adventure ever.

He hadn't been able to block Viridian's words out. They'd replayed constantly in his head, giving him a peculiar tingle of excitement.

'Well, I'm sure it's him,' Dad was insisting. 'The kid needs a good kick up his green backside. Anyway, who's he calling Polluters? I recycle, don't I, if I remember?'

Jay shook his head. 'Verdans think humans are polluting the planet just by existing, just by *breathing*.'

'Well, what are they going to do about it? They can't wipe us out.'

Jay kept quiet. He was thinking about Viridian's alien eyes and the deep green fires inside them. Viridian's absolute certainty that being Verdan was the only choice.

'Anyway, I thought Verdans never cause trouble?' said Dad, as if he was reading Jay's mind. 'Why's this Viridian kid so different?'

Jay's mobile rang before he could answer. It was inside the Diner and he ran to answer it. Dad called after him, 'If that's the school, you can tell them to shove it!'

The new term had started, but Dad had told the school Jay was sick. They kept phoning up, demanding doctor's notes. But Jay had wild dreams of never going back. He saw his future differently now, as a young entrepreneur. He and Dad would build up a business together. They'd have Diners all along the motorway. Rainbirds Diners would go national, global! And he and Dad would be millionaires.

But it wasn't the school on the phone. It was Gran.

Jay answered, and immediately started apologizing. Gran only lived a mile away in Franklin, and she had brought Jay up, looking after him when Dad was away. But since Dad had come back, and they started up the Diner, Jay hadn't been to see her.

'Sorry, Gran,' he gabbled into the phone. 'We've been really busy here at the Diner.'

Jay was lying. The truth was that, in the last few weeks, business had gone scarily slack. Because of Dad's sign no Verdans had stopped. That wouldn't have mattered if the human truckers had kept coming. But the big delivery lorries they drove were disappearing fast from the motorway. And many of the remaining truckers were Verdans.

'Gran, I've been meaning to come and see you,' Jay went on. 'I'll come as soon as I can, I promise.'

Jay steeled himself for a telling off. But Gran wasn't mad at him. In fact she sounded really cheery. She said, 'Jay, I've got some good news. I've got the virus.'

'*What*?'

'I've got the virus,' repeated Gran. 'I'm a Verdan now.'

'How'd that happen, Gran?' squawked Jay, his voice cracked with shock and disbelief. 'Were you gardening? I *told* you to be careful!'

'It wasn't an accident,' said Gran. 'I had the injection. And it's the best thing I ever did. My arthritis has disappeared, no pain or stiffness at all...'

Jay wasn't listening. He raced out to Dad, the phone clutched in his hand. 'Gran's got the virus,' he panted. She got herself injected with it.'

Dad grabbed the phone and barked into it, 'Have you lost your mind?'

But Gran had ended the call.

'Right,' said Dad. 'We're going round there, see what this nonsense is all about.'

Jay said, 'Do you think that's a good idea, Dad? We'll have to close the Diner.'

Dad was already in a bad mood, because of the damage to his precious Silver Bullet. And he didn't get on with Gran anyway. Gran was Jay's mum's mum. Mum had died after a crash when she was riding pillion on Dad's motorbike, and Gran blamed Dad.

Dad was already on the way to the van, and Jay had to sprint to keep up with him. Dad leapt into the driving seat, Jay scrambled in beside him and with a screech of tyres they roared off, towards Franklin.

They had to pass Jay's school. Jay got ready to duck down in his seat. But then he saw he didn't need to. There were a few cars in the car park but no school buses, no kids pouring up the drive.

Jay thought, *Where is everybody?*

They passed the Agricultural Research Station on the right, its three huge glass eco-domes set back from the road behind trees. As usual, a Security Guard sat in a little hut just inside the entrance and lifted barriers to let vehicles in and out. Jay was surprised to see that he was a Verdan.

But he didn't have time to think about that because Dad was pulling onto Gran's estate. They skidded to a stop in front of her house.

As Jay got out, he suddenly felt the back of his neck prickle. His head whisked round and, in the house opposite, he saw a green hand let a curtain fall.

Dad had gone striding up the garden path. Now he was hammering on Gran's front door. More curtains twitched in the houses across the road.

'I've got a key,' Jay said quickly. He let them both inside.

The house was very silent and still. The air smelled stale.

Gran wasn't downstairs. Jay clattered up the stairs yelling 'Gran!' He flung open bedroom doors and noticed, with a sudden pang, that Gran had kept his bedroom just as he left it, weeks ago, when he'd gone to live with Dad. As if she thought Jay might soon be coming back.

'She's probably out in the garden,' Jay told himself.

Gran was a mad-keen gardener and spent ages outside, weeding and lopping off straggly bits of plants.

'*Whoa!*' said Jay as he pushed open the back door. Over the summer, since he'd been away, Gran's garden had gone berserk. It was more like the wilderness around the Silver

Bullet than Gran's neat and tidy plot. Big tough weeds had taken over, suffocating smaller plants. Yellow slimy toadstools had killed the grass on her lawn. Spiny brambles crept over the ground, hooking themselves into her hedges, strangling her tender flowers.

It just wasn't like Gran to let her garden get out of control like this.

'Gran?' shouted Jay as he pushed his way through the weeds. Dad was behind him, but he had gone quiet, as if he was nervous about what they would find.

'You out here?' called Jay. A bramble looped round his leg. Jay swore. Had it scratched him? Then a green hand slid out of some tall purple thistles, and Jay yelled out in alarm.

'It's only me,' said Gran, and as Jay stood, frozen, she squatted down, disentangled the bramble and freed it. Jay saw how quickly and easily she moved now, how supple she was, like a cat.

'Hi, sweetheart,' she said to Jay. Then her eyes slid away again, as if she wasn't that interested.

Jay stared at her Verdan face, her green skin, clammy with water drops, her hair fluffed out around her head like green candyfloss. She wasn't Gran any more. She was one of *them*.

He couldn't find a single thing to say.

Gran had moved away to find some sunlight. She was soaking up the rays, her eyes closed as if she was in a trance.

Dad wasn't speechless. He stuck his fierce face into Gran's. 'What did you do this for?' he demanded.

Gran said serenely, 'Do you mind moving back a bit, you're shading my light.' Then, ignoring Dad, she added, 'Join us, Jay. Get the injection.'

'I can't believe I'm hearing this,' said Dad.

'It's the right thing to do,' she continued, calmly. 'I feel so at peace. It's such a pure and beautiful way to live.'

'Stop preaching all that Verdan crap,' said Dad. 'He doesn't want to know.'

Jay knew this was heading for a storm. Every time Dad and Gran met, it started off politely enough, for Jay's sake. But sooner or later, they'd forget about Jay and end up screaming at each other.

Dad would shout, 'You never give me a chance, do you?' Gran would call him a loser, Dad would call her an old witch. Then, always, it would end with that terrible accusation: 'If my daughter hadn't met you, she'd be alive now.' And Dad would yell, 'You *know* it wasn't my fault!' Then he'd go slamming furiously out the door.

Jay loved Gran. She'd always been there when Dad hadn't. She was reliable, solid as a rock. But he loved his wayward dad too.

'How could you do this?' Dad was fuming at Gran. 'Become one of those green freaks, spouting their crazy propaganda!'

Gran's response was worse than any row. She just moved off to find a sunnier spot, as though she'd forgotten them. As if Jay didn't matter any more.

But there was something Gran did care about. As she was sliding off into the greenery, she pounced, with horrible cat-like quickness, on an upturned plastic bucket.

Gran lifted it up. Underneath was a sick-looking pot plant. Instead of being bristling and bright green, it was pale yellow with a long floppy stem and two droopy yellow leaves.

'Oh, no!' Gran seemed really upset.

'What's the matter, Gran?' said Jay. But Gran didn't even glance in his direction.

'Poor little etiolated plant,' she crooned. 'Growing in the dark like that! No wonder you're poorly. Never mind, we'll find you a nice patch of sunlight.'

And she went off, cradling the plant and talking to it tenderly.

Instantly Jay's mind flashed back to when he was about three years old. He'd had tonsillitis, it hurt to swallow. His throat felt like it was full of barbed wire. Gran had gone specially to the supermarket to get him chocolate ice cream. She'd said, 'We'll soon make you better.' Then she'd fed him the ice cream, spoon by spoon.

'Gran,' whispered Jay forlornly, gazing after her.

Now he felt really scared. In his heart, he simply didn't trust Dad to look after him. Dad never had before. But, until now, there had always been Gran.

Dad grabbed him. 'Come on,' he said. 'We're not staying here. She might try to give you the virus.'

Jay took a last look back. But, in all that green, he couldn't tell which was the garden and which was Gran.

In the van, Jay found himself thinking forbidden thoughts again. Would it really be so bad to be a Verdan? He'd never seen Gran looking so calm and healthy and happy.

If we were all Verdans, thought Jay, *there'd be no more rows. We'd all get on really well. And we'd be saving the planet at the same time.*

But there was no way Jay could confess his thoughts to Dad. Dad was saying, 'It's like she's a robot, brainwashed or something. One thing's for sure. You can't live with her any more.'

'But I don't need to, do I?' Jay said, with sudden panic. 'I'm living with *you*, aren't I? That's the plan, isn't it?'

Dad looked a bit flustered. 'Er, yes, of course. That's the plan.'

'You aren't going to go away again?'

'No, I'm not,' said Dad, defensively. 'I told you, I'm here to stay.'

Jay had heard that before. But this time, he almost believed it. Something seemed to have changed in Dad's mind. As though he had to take his responsibilities seriously now. Because he suddenly said, 'You'd better go back to school.'

'Why?' said Jay, astonished.

'Because if you don't, they might put me in jail for not sending you. I heard they do that nowadays. And then what would you do?'

'I could keep the Diner going,' said Jay desperately. 'I'd be all right there on my own.'

'No,' said Dad. 'I'm taking you back to school. Right now.'

CHAPTER 4

They drove, in tense silence, back to Franklin High School by way of Franklin High Street.

Jay gazed out at the shops. Franklin's two takeaways had closed down. A new place called The Mineral Café had opened up. It was crowded with Verdans, sitting at outside tables, with tall glasses of blue and milky white drinks.

Jay read the board outside the café. 'Get your Nutrients Here,' it said. 'Today's Special: Phosphorus Pick Me Up.'

Dad frowned. 'What's that all about?'

'Verdans don't need human food,' said Jay patiently. 'Only light, water and minerals.'

'But what about humans?' said Dad. 'Don't they come down here any more?'

'There's some, Dad,' said Jay. 'And, look, there's some more over there.' But mostly, the High Street seemed like a green sea of Verdans.

Dad drove on, grim-faced.

Jay said, 'Maybe we should change Rainbirds American Diner to Rainbirds Mineral Drinks.'

'If that's supposed to be a joke, it isn't funny.'

Jay didn't dare tell Dad that he'd never felt more serious in his life.

Then Dad suddenly braked, shouting, 'Jay, look! That kid over there, isn't that Sage?'

Jay squinted at the Verdan girl, skipping along in a world of her own. 'I think so. Yeah.'

'Bet she knows where Viridian is,' said Dad. 'Go on, get out and ask her.'

'What, me?' said Jay.

'Yes, you. I'm not going anywhere near that freaky kid. Go on.'

At first Sage didn't seem to notice Jay. She tried to skip around him as though he was a litter bin on the pavement.

Jay blocked her way. He wasn't sure what to say.

'You on your own?' he started. 'Where are your mum and dad?'

Sage shrugged. 'They've gone away.' She didn't seem at all distressed.

Jay said, 'Have they left you on your own?' Sage stared at him, as if she didn't understand the question.

How did you get through to this kid? Jay tried a different approach. 'Remember me? From the Diner? I helped your brother get you down from the ivy.'

'You're shading my light,' she said.

Jay decided to get to the point. 'Where's Viridian?'

'Who?' she said, lifting her face to the sun and smiling.

'Your brother,' said Jay. 'Remember him?'

Sage said, 'Oh, he's gone away too.' She waved vaguely over the rooftops. 'To the building with glass bubbles.'

'What?'

'Three glass bubbles,' said Sage, untangling her long, green hair. 'Great big ones you can walk into.'

'You mean the Agricultural Research Station?'

Sage shrugged again. 'He's gone to be a Cultivar.' She peered at Jay through her river weed hair. 'I painted words on your caravan.'

'Excuse me?'

'I painted words on your caravan,' Sage repeated, as if she was pleased with herself.

Jay stared at her open-mouthed. Sage was a weird little Verdan. But he'd thought she was harmless.

'Why'd you do that?' he asked.

'Because I'm going to be a Cultivar. And Viridian says, to be a Cultivar you must hate Polluters.' Sage smiled at Jay, coyly twisting her hair round a long green finger. 'I'm already in the Climbers.'

Jay was totally bewildered now. 'What's the Climbers?'

'It's for Verdans who've been chosen to be Cultivars one day. It's where we learn how to hate Polluters.'

She pointed at him with a twiggy arm, her finger outstretched. 'You are a Polluter,' she chirped cheerfully at him. 'So you must die!'

Jay gaped. She smiled at him again.

'When I told the other Climbers what I'd done, they said, "Well done, Sage, you will make an excellent Cultivar one day." And they gave me my orange belt to show I'd passed a test, and some extra sunshine.'

'What?' said Jay. 'What are you talking about? Extra sunshine?'

But Sage said, 'I'm not supposed to talk to Polluters.' Then she darted off, swift as a dragonfly.

Jay stood on the pavement, staring after her. He gave one quick, convulsive shiver. Then he climbed back in the van.

'Did she say where he is?' asked Dad eagerly.

'No,' said Jay. 'She doesn't know.'

Dad swore and started up the engine.

Jay didn't like lying to Dad, but something told him that Viridian was nothing but trouble. That they should stay right away from him.

But he did say, 'You were wrong about Viridian. It was Sage that did the graffiti.'

'You're kidding me.'

'She just told me,' said Jay. 'She did it to win an orange belt and extra sunshine.'

'What?'

Jay shrugged. 'It's what she told me.'

Dad was quiet for a minute. Then he said, 'She's a creepy kid, isn't she?'

Jay didn't answer. He was thinking about those chilling words, 'You must die!' coming from a young girl's mouth.

Then he told himself, *Don't take it so seriously. She didn't understand what she was saying.*

'Do I turn right here?' asked Dad, who'd never been to Jay's school before.

Jay tried to adjust his mind as they approached the school. It would be weird seeing his friends again. They must have thought he'd fallen off the planet. Since he'd been at the Diner with Dad he hadn't contacted any of them, hadn't answered their texts. He'd thought his time at school was over and done with: they were kids, messing about in the classroom, while he was in the real world, growing up fast.

But, suddenly, he was quite looking forward to seeing them.

They were in a stream of cars now, heading for Franklin High. Dad followed them through the big iron gates.

Then Jay saw the sign. 'Look, Dad!'

The sign said, 'GET YOUR PLANT VIRUS SHOTS HERE'.

'What's going on?' said Dad. 'I'm going to turn round.' But he couldn't; he was stuck in a stream of cars.

In the school car park there were Verdan kids in high visibility jackets, waving cars into free parking spaces. With a sudden chill, Jay realized they were students at his school. 'That's Lily Mae Taylor,' he said. 'And that's Rashid. I'm going to find out what's going on.'

'Wait,' said Dad.

But Jay had already leapt out of the van. He fought his way through the crowds of people, all heading for the main entrance.

'Hey!' he greeted Lily Mae, trying not to stare at her pea-green braided hair.

'Where have you been?' she asked him, without much interest. 'No-one's seen you for ages.'

She spoke like the old Lily Mae, but Jay only had to look into the depths of her vivid green eyes to know she was a stranger.

'You here to get injected?' asked Lily Mae.

'I don't like needles,' said Jay.

'It's just a little sting,' said Lily Mae, showing her green teeth in a grin. 'Everyone's doing it. All my Facebook friends are Verdans. Aren't yours?'

Jay said, 'We're not on the Net where I live now.'

The world had moved on but he'd been left behind. He thought, incredulously: *I'm the odd one out and they're normal.*

But then his best friend, Mac, came racing up. With a huge surge of relief Jay saw he wasn't a Verdan. He was still the same old crazy Mac.

'Hey, Mac!' shouted Jay. 'Am I glad to see you. I thought I was the only human left!'

Mac turned round. His face was flushed with excitement.

'They can't stop me now,' he said. 'Stupid Polluters, living in the past.'

‘Who can’t stop you?’ asked Jay.

‘My parents,’ said Mac. ‘They can’t tell me what to do. I’m getting a virus shot whether they like it or not.’

‘My dad won’t let me,’ said Jay. ‘He hates Verdans.’

‘So does mine,’ said Mac. He gave that shrill giggle that Jay had heard so often in class. ‘What are they going to do about it? Wipe us all out? Come on!’

Mac grabbed his arm, and Jay found himself caught up in the crowd of eager, smiling humans heading for the school hall.

Jay expected a sickly antiseptic smell and queues of silent, shuffling people, wincing as they got jabbed. But it wasn’t like that at all.

The hall was flooded with sunshine from the big tall windows. And the atmosphere was joyous. People were dancing and having fun. The school steel band was playing. The hall was decorated with green flags and streamers.

Jay detached himself from the crowd and hung back to watch.

It was like a party, but the weirdest, craziest party Jay had ever seen. People were jostling to get their jabs from Verdan nurses, rolling up their sleeves as if they could hardly wait. It was obviously much quicker and more effective than catching the virus from live plant sap. Within minutes, a green tinge began to show around the injection spot. In hours the same thing would happen all over your body. But as soon as they saw that hint of green, people whooped with joy. Verdans crowded around them: 'Welcome! You're one of us now.'

And Jay, slumped against the wall, felt left out, a sad, lonely Polluter. Self-pity flooded through him. And sneaky thoughts were forming in his head. 'Why should Dad tell you what to do? It's *your* future.'

That made him remember Viridian's words. 'We are the Future. Becoming a Cultivar – it's the biggest adventure ever.'

The biggest adventure. The biggest adventure. The words danced in his head to the rhythm of the steel drums.

A Verdan was up on the stage. Jay saw, without much surprise, that it was the Head Teacher of Franklin High.

The Head said, 'Franklin High is proud to be host to this happy event. There was a time when the Earth was inhabited only by plants. Our world was Paradise, before animals came along to pollute it and steal its resources. Because of your brave choice today, our planet will be healed and made beautiful again! Together we shall turn our backs on our misguided, modern lives. We will go back to that purer, simpler way of life and make our Earth a Paradise once more!'

Wild clapping and cheering followed this speech. Jay found himself joining in.

Mac came racing up, euphoric. 'It doesn't hurt at all,' he shouted above the din. 'Well, it does a bit. But it's worth it.'

Jay found himself grinning too, yelling, 'Well done, mate, I'm pleased for you.'

'I've chosen a new name,' said Mac, his eyes shining fervently. Already they seemed to have a greenish tint. 'You've got to call me Thorn from now on.'

Dad would have made a joke. Jay said, 'Nice one, Thorn,' and slapped the brand-new Verdan on the back.

'Come on!' said Mac – Thorn – and suddenly Jay was surrounded by Verdans, gently guiding him towards the nurses, full of encouraging words. 'Join us and be happy. Make Paradise on Earth. It's brilliant, it's the best thing you'll ever do.'

Jay let himself be carried along. He forgot about Dad and his own fears. *The biggest adventure ever*, his brain kept repeating. *Paradise on Earth.*

Then all he could hear in his head was the music. And, before he knew it, he was staring down at the tiny puncture wound in his left arm, waiting for it to bleach to grey, then show the first signs of green.

The world seemed to stand still. Minutes passed.

Thorn said, in a baffled voice, 'Nothing's happening.'

The Verdan nurse bustled round the table and inspected Jay's arm.

'You don't seem to have got the virus,' she told Jay. 'It can't be the serum. It's worked for everyone else.'

Quickly, the word spread and people waiting for their shots crowded round, confused, asking questions, staring at Jay as if he was a circus freak. Thorn seemed to have melted away.

Doors flew open at the end of the hall. The crashing noise startled Jay, and the band stopped playing. Verdans were pushing through the throng towards him. They were taller and darker green than the others. They looked tougher, like bouncers or bodyguards. And they stalked through the throng in a super-confident, swaggering way.

'*Cultivars*,' Jay heard a Verdan whisper.

Other Verdans, even the nurses, shrank away, leaving Jay standing alone.

The Cultivars made a circle around him, facing outwards, blocking out the light. Jay began to feel very scared.

One announced loudly, 'Nothing to worry about, Verdans. We'll take care of this. Carry on with the virus shots.'

The band started up again. Outside the circle that imprisoned him, Jay heard people celebrating, as if nothing was happening.

He said, 'What's going on?'

No-one answered. Then one of the Cultivars slowly twisted his neck and stared at Jay.

It was Viridian. His eyes glittered like a green, icy pond. 'It's you,' he said. He seemed astonished to see Jay was still human. 'I made you a Verdan. We mixed blood.'

The Cultivar next to Viridian leaned over and hissed something to him. Immediately Viridian turned his face away, as if Jay had ceased to exist.

'What's going on?' Jay stammered again. Now he was getting really panicky.

Then the circle started moving. Jay was forced to move with it.

'Where are you taking me?' he asked, his voice shrill now, almost hysterical.

No-one answered.

Then, from somewhere in the hall, he heard Dad bellow, 'Jay, where are you?'

'Dad! Over here!' Jay screamed. He threw himself at the circle, battering against his captors, frantic to find a way through. But they closed together, squeezing Jay into a smaller space. He stood panting, helpless, defeated.

Then, unbelievably, a gap showed between a Cultivar's legs. Jay made a mad dive for it, slithering through like a snake.

One of his captors yelled a warning: 'He's escaping!'

Jay heard Viridian's voice: 'Let him go. We'll get him later. I know where he lives.'

Jay was running blindly now, bouncing off Verdans, shoving them aside trying to find an exit from the hall.

'Dad!' he yelled, as he ran. 'Dad!'

And then Dad appeared from nowhere, grabbing Jay's arm, dragging him out of the hall.

'They're after me,' gasped Jay as they ran across the car park.

They leapt into the van. Dad screeched out of the car park, forcing incoming cars to swerve out of his way.

Jay looked back, sure they would be pursued. But there

was no sign of any Cultivars among the happy stream of humans going in to get their shots.

'Don't think they're following us,' said Jay. 'Dad, I couldn't get out. They wouldn't let me go.'

Dad said, 'What were you doing in there anyway?' He floored the accelerator as they sped back to the Silver Bullet.

Jay didn't want to explain that. 'Those were Cultivars, Dad, the ones around me. Viridian was with them. They were really scary.'

'Come on,' scoffed Dad. 'Whatever they call themselves, they're still Verdans. Verdans aren't scary. They're wimps.'

'Not this lot,' said Jay. 'They're different. Believe me.'

CHAPTER 5

Jay and Dad were sitting in the Silver Bullet eating burgers for supper. There were no customers. Since they got back from Franklin that morning, not a single trucker had stopped at the Diner.

Jay said, 'So are we going to see Gran again?'

Dad said, 'I'm not. You can, if you like.'

Jay frowned. He wasn't sure Gran wanted to see *him*. When people became Verdans they didn't seem to need family anymore. It seemed really selfish to Jay. But weren't they supposed to be saving the world?

Dad said, 'So what actually happened in that school hall? You haven't really told me.'

Jay didn't want to tell Dad that he'd willingly gone to get his virus shot. He chose his words very carefully.

'I got caught up in the crowd. Before I knew, it they'd given me the shot. I couldn't help it, Dad.'

'Hey, it wasn't your fault. So when nothing happened, like the shot didn't work, these Cultivars appeared out of nowhere?'

'Yeah. They surrounded me, tried to take me away. It was like they were arresting me or something.'

'But you escaped,' said Dad. 'That's my boy!'

'But why didn't the shot work? Why didn't I get the virus? I didn't get it before either, when Viridian tried to infect me.'

'You've got the luck of the devil, that's all I can say. That's twice those green freaks have nearly made you one of them.'

It was time for the news. Dad flicked on the TV. 'Hey, look at this!' he said.

The Prime Minister and his wife and children were standing outside Number 10 Downing Street, smiling. They had green chlorophyll skin.

Jay gaped in amazement. 'They've become Verdans!'

'I don't believe this,' said Dad. 'When did this happen? Wait a minute, he's saying something.'

'After much consideration,' the Prime Minister was saying, 'my family and I have decided that being Verdan is the obvious, indeed the only choice. We've been given an opportunity to put things right and repair the damage that we have done as humans. We must seize that opportunity! My ministers and other world leaders agree with me. This is a global movement. A chance for people, of whatever creed or colour, to join together to become new, purer life forms, and save our planet!'

There was wild cheering in the background.

Other photos were flashed up on the screen of leaders across the world, entire governments, who'd all become Verdans.

Then there were interviews with Verdans on the street, in London.

'Of course,' said a Verdan woman, 'it's everyone's free choice, and I'm not prejudiced against humans. And we'll never *force* anyone. But I *do* want to say this to anyone who's still human: How can you carry on polluting the planet with your waste products, breathing CO_2 into the atmosphere? It's dirty and selfish...'

Dad switched off the programme, snorting in disgust. 'Looks like we're the bad guys now, son. It's me and you against the world.'

Jay said, 'Look, Dad, maybe she's got a point – '

'*What?* Are you turning against me too?'

'I'm just saying! Why can't we even *talk* about it?'

'I bet you're disappointed, really, aren't you?' shouted Dad. 'That those two chances you had of going Verdan didn't work!'

Jay threw down his half-eaten burger and got up.

'Where are you going?' demanded Dad.

'I'm going to get the sign. Time to close up.' Jay walked out of the Diner.

Dad yelled after him, 'You're coming back, aren't you?' To Jay's surprise, Dad's voice sounded suddenly desperately lonely and insecure.

'Course I'm coming back,' Jay told him. 'Where else can I go?'

Jay carried the 'OPEN' sign back up the slip road. The setting sun washed the whole landscape with a fiery glow. The tangled weeds and tall grasses of their little plot seemed to be burning.

A green hand shot out of the vegetation and seized Jay's wrist.

Jay dropped the sign. 'Get off!' He tried to twist himself free.

Viridian slithered out of the bushes. 'Shhh,' he said. 'Your lives are in danger. They're coming. Be quick.'

He dragged Jay towards the trailer, his grip like a vice. He seemed to have become taller, stronger. His skin had a glossy, dark green sheen, and he wore camouflage trousers and a green T-shirt.

Dad leapt up in surprise as the two of them almost fell in the door.

'You've got a cheek,' he spat, glaring furiously at Viridian. 'Showing your green face again around here. And what are you doing dressed like that? Think you're some kind of action man?'

Viridian stared Dad down contemptuously. He said, 'The Cultivars are coming. Jay's got about fifteen minutes to live. And they'll probably kill you too.'

'What?' said Dad, shocked out of his anger. 'Why do they want to kill Jay?'

'Because he's an Immune,' said Viridian. 'And all Immunes must be terminated.'

'An Immune,' echoed Jay, in a dazed voice.

'Yes, you can't catch the plant virus,' said Viridian, impatiently.

At last everything began to make sense. It wasn't because of antiseptic, or a dud batch of virus that he didn't get infected.

'I'm immune,' Jay repeated, in an awed voice.

'But *why* do they want to kill him?' persisted Dad.

'Look, there's no time for all this now,' Viridian said, urgently. 'Just take my word for it. If you don't do as I say, you're both going to die.'

Dad opened his mouth to argue.

'Just listen to him, Dad,' Jay begged.

'I persuaded the Cultivars to let me go ahead, scout around,' Viridian went on. 'But they're not far behind. They'll be here soon – '

Dad interrupted. 'Why should we believe you? You're one of them, aren't you? This could be a trap.'

Viridian turned to Jay. 'Do you think you'd have escaped this morning if it hadn't been for me? I let you out of the circle. I made sure you weren't pursued. Blood brothers, remember. Even if you are an Immune.'

Jay's guts felt like water. He was in an agony of indecision. Did he trust Viridian or didn't he?

He stared into Viridian's eyes. Their depths glittered, with pure green fire that seemed almost sacred. Jay had to tear his own eyes away.

And he suddenly found that he'd made up his mind.

'I believe him, Dad. He's here to help us.'

Dad muttered something they couldn't make out. Then he said, 'OK. I'm listening.'

'Right,' said Viridian. 'You'll have to blow up the Silver Bullet.'

'What?' said Dad, outraged. 'You must be joking.'

'The only way to survive,' said Viridian, 'is if I can convince the Cultivars you're dead. You have to blow up the trailer, drive away, find somewhere to hide. I'll tell them you died in the explosion.'

'I'm not going to blow up my trailer,' said Dad. 'It cost me every penny I've got. If they're coming, we'll defend it. We'll fight them off.'

'Don't be stupid,' said Viridian. 'There's twenty of us at least.'

'How many?' said Dad, appalled.

'Twenty,' repeated Viridian. 'They're coming across the fields from the Research Station.'

'We don't stand a chance, Dad,' said Jay.

'Look, if you want to save Jay's life, you have to act now,' said Viridian. 'Once they're here, there's nothing I can do to stop them. They'll kill him immediately, no question.'

'Will they have guns?' asked Dad.

'No, we don't believe in them. We're working on proper

Verdan weapons. But even without them, Cultivars can easily deal with two puny humans.'

Dad didn't even react to the insult. The thought of blowing up the Silver Bullet was more than he could bear. He appealed to Jay one last time. 'You sure you believe him? I just don't see why – '

Viridian interrupted. 'Stop wasting time. If they don't think he's dead they'll hunt him down. He's an Immune. Wherever he goes, they'll find him.'

'If we just tow the trailer, go far enough away from Franklin...'

Viridian flashed Dad a scornful look. 'There are Cultivars all over the world,' he said. 'A network, in contact all the time. We're getting ready to take control. We'll take the Verdan revolution to new heights.'

Dad stared into Viridian's fanatical green eyes. 'What the hell does all that *mean*?'

'Look, there's only one question for you to worry about,' said Viridian. 'Do you want to save your son's life or don't you?'

Dad gave a deep, grieving sigh, as if he'd finally realized there was no other way. Then, at last, he sprang into action.

'Jay, load up the van. Take all the food you can find. Not the freezer stuff. Cans of stuff we can eat cold. And soft drinks.'

While Dad raced back into the Silver Bullet, grabbing clothes, duvets, anything else they might need, Jay filled his arms with cans from the shipping container: beans, sardines, canned fruit, custard. He came staggering back to the van to dump it in, then made the same trip again and again.

Viridian didn't help. He stood gazing out towards Franklin over fields flushed red by the light of the dying sun.

'No time to load any more,' he said. 'They're coming.'

At first, Dad and Jay could only make out a green blur in the distance, a mile or so away. It looked like trees. But then those trees began to move. They were Cultivars. Like alien invaders, they came marching across the fields.

'Come on, Dad,' said Jay. 'We have to go.'

Dad drove the van to the slip road. He raced back, and got a big can of petrol out of the generator building.

'I'll do it, Dad,' said Jay.

'No,' ordered Dad, in a choked voice. 'Go and sit in the van. Start it up.'

Jay sat in the van with the engine running and watched Dad, through the open door of the Diner, pouring petrol everywhere.

Viridian ran to the van, in an easy, wolf-like lope. Jay opened the window.

'Give me your phone,' ordered Viridian. 'I'll contact the leader, delay them a few minutes.'

Jay handed over his mobile. Then Viridian was gone, diving into the green wilderness around the edge of their plot.

Dad hurried back to the van, walking backwards, pouring

a steady stream of petrol. Then he knelt down, sparked a match and lit the petrol. Flames flared up and went speeding along the petrol trail towards the Silver Bullet. Dad leapt in the van.

'I left the gas taps wide open,' he told Jay.

The stove was fuelled with propane gas. When the petrol flames ignited the gas there'd be an almighty bang.

Dad took a last quick glance back. Then they were speeding down the slip road.

They were on the motorway when the Silver Bullet went up. Even in the van, they heard the muffled boom. In the van mirrors, they saw a brilliant white fireball behind them in the evening sky, then a pillar of black smoke rising and spreading out into a mushroom cloud.

For a few minutes, neither of them spoke.

Then Jay said, 'Dad, I'm really sorry.'

'I don't want to talk about it, OK?'

They drove on in silence. Dad gripping the steering wheel with bone-white knuckles, staring grimly ahead.

Finally, Jay said, 'Dad, where are we going?'

Dad's voice, when he finally answered, was quiet. He said, 'Not far. What's the point if there are Cultivars wherever we go?'

'So where are we going then?'

'Somewhere dark,' answered Dad. 'Verdans hate the dark.'

A minute later, he added, 'Did I hear that green freak

right? Did he say something about you and him being blood brothers?'

'No, Dad,' said Jay, his nerves jumping even more than they were already. 'He didn't say anything like that.'

Dad let the subject drop. Jay breathed a sigh of relief.

* * *

The Cultivars crowded around the crater where the Silver Bullet had exploded. Wispy smoke rose from its black, skeletal remains at the bottom of the gaping pit. Smouldering debris and glass shards lay scattered among the chairs and tables. The 'OPEN. Best Burgers in England' sign had been blown into a tree.

The generator building had gone up too. Bricks had been hurled all over the Rainbirds' plot. Only the shipping container was still standing, its metal sides scorched black by the ferocious heat.

Viridian stood with the Cultivar's leader, Teal. She was the one who'd recruited him for the Cultivar programme. She'd approached him on the streets, soon after he'd become a Verdan.

She'd said, 'I'm from an elite group of Verdans called Cultivars. We aren't content just to have chlorophyll skin. We want to take being Verdan to its furthest limits. Want to join us?'

And Viridian had said, immediately, 'Count me in.'

Viridian had excelled as a Climber, a trainee Cultivar. The small doses of artificial sunshine he'd been allowed while training had sharpened his aggression, made him hungry for more. In record time he'd won his purple belt and been made a Cultivar.

Then things had really started happening.

Teal and the Verdan scientists carried out experiments on Viridian and the other Cultivars. They had changed Viridian's body with extra sunlight and gene therapy, making him greener, taller, stronger than other Verdans. But they had also changed his mind. Verdans were gentle and peaceable. But Cultivars were as tough and competitive as the world's most successful plants. Plants like Japanese knotweed. Or nettles. Or bramble that stole other plants' nutrients, shaded them from the life-giving sun, strangled and killed them with its spiny arms so it alone could thrive.

Viridian had known for a while that he'd have to get rid of Teal. Once she was out of the way, he'd take her place as Franklin's top Cultivar. And that was only the start of his ambitions.

But until today, he hadn't been sure how to eliminate her. Not until he'd realised Jay gave him the perfect way to do it.

'Looks like a gas explosion,' said Teal looking down into the crater. 'Was it an accident? Nobody could have survived that.'

'That's what we're supposed to think,' said Viridian.

'That it was an accident. That they died in the blast. But go and search in the wreckage. You won't find their bodies.'

'So what happened?' said another Cultivar.

'I saw them, the Immune and his father,' said Viridian. 'They rigged up the trailer to explode. Then they escaped in a van. I would've stopped them but I had to take cover.' He addressed the crowd of Cultivars. 'The thing is, either they were really lucky, escaping in the nick of time. Or someone warned the Immune we were coming.'

'Warned an Immune?' said Teal. 'Who would do that? You're not saying it was one of us?'

'I've suspected for a while,' said Viridian, 'that there are spies among us. Immune sympathisers.'

'Immune sympathisers? That's madness,' said Teal. 'We all know Immunes must be killed. Or else everything we've gained will be lost.'

'But that's just what some of us secretly wish for,' said Viridian in silky smooth tones. 'To go back to the bad old days.'

The other Cultivars looked sideways at each other. They were murmuring doubtfully. But Viridian was powerful, a brilliant rising star. No one dared cross him.

Except Teal.

'I don't believe it,' she burst out, her green eyes fiery. 'I'm senior to you, Viridian. I recruited you. I won't have you spreading dangerous rumours. Be quiet, unless you have proof that one of us warned him!'

'Oh, I have proof,' said Viridian, softly. 'It's here, on the Immune's phone. He dropped it, as they were escaping.'

He held up Jay's mobile for them to see. 'The traitor's number is on this phone, showing they were in contact. He also texted her about twenty minutes ago, to tell her everything had gone according to plan.'

'Her?' said Teal.

She gazed into Viridian's triumphant eyes, then looked at the number on the screen of the phone he held. And for the first time, she began to feel afraid.

She grabbed her mobile from the pocket of her combat trousers. It had been switched off, like all the Cultivars' phones, as they marched over the fields.

She switched it on.

'I think you'll find,' said Viridian, as he snatched the phone from her, 'that the Immune's message is in your inbox.'

'That's no proof!' said Teal. Her voice sounded desperate. She saw that the Cultivars had moved away as if they didn't want to be contaminated. Now she was standing alone.

'I have much more proof,' said Viridian. Every Cultivar was quiet, listening. He had them hooked. 'It's on your laptop back at the Research Station. All sorts of sickening stuff about how Immunes must be saved and the virus must be eliminated.'

'You've hacked into my computer,' whispered Teal. 'I didn't write that.'

She realized, with a flash of pure terror, that she'd totally underestimated what a dangerous and ruthless rival Viridian was. But it was too late now.

'No more lies,' said Viridian. He turned his eyes, glowing with conviction, to the other Cultivars. 'Arrest the traitor.'

Two Cultivars moved alongside Teal. Each grasped one of her arms.

'What about the Immune?' asked another Cultivar.

'Catch him and kill him. Death to all Immunes. Now I'm in charge here, things will change. There'll be nowhere for Immunes to hide.'

'And what about spies and Immune Sympathisers?' asked the other Cultivar.

'They must be Etiolated,' said Viridian. 'Without mercy.'

CHAPTER 6

Dad drove like a maniac. It was lucky there weren't any police cars about. In fact, there wasn't much traffic at all.

'Where are all the lorries?' said Jay, gazing down the eerily empty motorway. He was worried for about two seconds because truck drivers were their main customers. Until he remembered that Rainbirds Diner didn't exist any more.

Dad said, 'There's no lorries because there's no deliveries. Businesses all over the world must be going bust. What do Verdans need to buy? Nothing.'

'Except minerals,' said Jay, pointing to a tanker trundling down a slip road. It said, 'NITRATES' on the side.

'They don't even need to buy those,' said Dad. 'They can get them by licking rocks. Get down!'

Dad took one hand off the wheel, slammed it on top of Jay's skull and shoved him down out of sight. 'It's OK, he's gone,' said he added after a minute, lifting his hand.

'What did you do that for?' said Jay, rubbing his head.

'That trucker was a Verdan. And those green freaks

want to kill you. I don't understand why. I don't understand anything any more.'

'But the Cultivars aren't after me now,' protested Jay. 'I'm dead, aren't I? They think we died in the explosion.'

'Yeah,' said Dad. 'That's provided Viridian told them, like he said he would.'

'Why don't you trust Viridian? He helped us, didn't he?'

'I don't trust any of those green freaks,' said Dad grimly. 'So far as I'm concerned it's us against them.'

Soon Dad turned off onto a side road, then another. Then the van was bouncing along a track, its wheels crunching on stones. They crossed hilly scrubland, dotted with gorse bushes and twisted, stunted trees. A misty twilight covered the landscape, making everything grey and blurred.

'Funny looking hills,' said Jay, just to break the silence. They were conical, with rounded tops, like hills a child would draw.

'They're not natural hills,' said Dad. 'They're old slag heaps.'

The van ground its way around them, rocked across a dry stream bed. Then Dad stopped. 'Here we are.'

They climbed out. The scrubland was silent, a desolate, lonely place, with no people or houses in sight.

In the side of a hill was a rusty iron grill, the size of a garage door. There was a tunnel behind it, big enough for the van to drive through. A sun-bleached sign on the grill said, 'DANGER! KEEP OUT!'

Jay peered through the grill. Near the entrance, ferns and mosses crowded the tunnel walls. Beyond that was blackness. But from somewhere he could hear water trickling.

'Hey!' He leapt back as something came streaking out and only just missed his head.

'A bat,' said Dad. 'This is an abandoned lead mine. It's full of them. When I was a boy me and my mates used to come here.' Dad chuckled to himself, which made Jay grin with relief. It was like Dad was fighting back at last. Jay was more worried about Dad right then than he was about himself.

'Yeah,' said Dad. 'There was a Danger sign there back then. We took no notice of it of course. We went in loads of times, explored every metre of that mine.'

Dad went up and pulled at the grill. It wouldn't move: it was stuck fast in the tunnel entrance. He frowned. 'This wasn't there back then,' he said. 'Here, Jay, help me.'

They both yanked at the grill. It wouldn't budge.

'We can't stay here,' said Jay, gazing round the darkening scrubland. It was suddenly very spooky out there.

Dad threw open the back of the van, rummaged inside. He tossed Jay a coiled towing rope.

'Here, tie that to the grill,' he said. 'Make sure it's tight.'

Dad looped the other end round the tow bar on the van. He leapt in and accelerated away. The van wheels skidded on rock as the rope tightened. The grill creaked and shifted.

'Keep going, Dad!' yelled Jay. 'It's moving!'

The van wheels screeched and spun wildly, churning up the dirt. The engine revved to a shrieking roar.

Jay thought, *Hope that rope holds. Hope the engine doesn't blow.*

Suddenly, the grill came crashing down. The sound echoed across the silent scrubland.

'Get in the van,' said Dad. He untied the tow rope. 'Can't see us getting that grill back in place. We'll disguise the entrance somehow. Stick the Danger sign up in front. Even if they *do* think you're dead, we don't want any Cultivar creeps finding out you're not.'

'How long will we have to hide out?' asked Jay.

'Until they've forgotten all about you,' said Dad. 'Or until our food runs out.'

He switched on the lights and drove the van slowly into the mine.

The van lights swept over crystals buried in the tunnel walls and made them glitter like silver.

'They used to have horses down here,' said Dad, 'to pull the wagons. We found horse shoes, me and my mates, loads of them, and old picks and sledge hammers.' He switched off the engine. 'We can't take the van any further.'

Jay got out of the van. The tunnel had opened out into a low chamber. Its walls were lost in darkness. But the headlamp beams lit up great timber posts supporting the roof. They stretched into the distance like the pillars down a cathedral aisle.

‘Wow,’ said Jay.

‘This is nothing,’ said Dad. ‘You’ll be amazed what’s down here.’

Jay’s foot clunked against something. ‘Hey,’ he said, ‘look what I found.’ It was a rusty old horse shoe.

‘That’s for luck,’ said Jay, holding it up in the light.

CHAPTER 7

Jay was lying in the back of the van, spooning cold baked beans out of a can. A lantern with a hand-driven dynamo cast a feeble yellow glow. Jay could have wound it up some more to get a brighter light. But he couldn't be bothered.

He yawned, and asked Dad, 'How long have we been down here?'

Dad shrugged. At first he'd counted the days but now he wasn't sure. 'Eight weeks?' he guessed. 'Couple of months?'

'It's longer than that!' protested Jay. To him, it felt like forever.

They were living like moles. They weren't entirely without light: they had torches and plenty of batteries, candles and the wind-up lanterns. And during the day some light, along with fresh air, filtered in from outside through the ventilation shafts.

Even so, it was miserably dark, and the air in the mine wasn't good. It smelt of wet rot down here, as if everything was decaying away. Jay was beginning to feel like some subterranean creature.

They were entirely cut off. Viridian had Jay's phone. Dad had never owned a mobile. But mobiles probably wouldn't have worked down here anyway.

Jay jerked his chin up towards the surface. 'Dad, what do you think is happening up there?'

'Who knows? Do you want to share some tinned peaches for afters?'

At first, they'd talked a lot about the surface. About whether there were any humans left up there in Franklin or whether the Verdans had totally taken over. About why Jay was Immune and why the Cultivars wanted all Immunes dead. About when it would be safe to leave the mine.

Dad's opinion was: 'It'll never be safe. But we'll have to take the chance soon. Our food supplies won't last forever.'

'So what do we do then?' Jay had asked.

'Go out and get more food. That old shipping container is probably still in one piece. There's lots of food left in there.'

Jay didn't think it was a good idea for Dad to go back, see his precious Silver Bullet a heap of mangled metal. He had suggested, 'We could ask Viridian for help. He helped us before.' But Dad had got angry, yelling, 'Why do you trust that green freak so much?'

So, gradually, they'd stopped talking so much about the surface world. As days slipped away the surface began to seem more and more unreal to Jay. As if they'd imagined everything that had happened up there, or it was some dreadful, surreal nightmare they'd shared. They found it better to drift, switch off their minds, take one day at a time. That way, you didn't go insane.

Once Dad had even said, 'When we go up, maybe everything will be back to normal. No more green freaks.'

Jay had agreed, 'Yeah, bet you're right.'

But, even if that somehow miraculously happened, the Silver Bullet would still be in bits. There'd be no family home and no business. That particular dream had gone up in smoke.

Dad just didn't want to face the truth. And down here, it was easy not to.

They'd got a sort of routine to their underground life. They ate, slept a lot, collected water. And they explored the mine. Dad took Jay on journeys of discovery to all the bits of the mine he'd explored as a boy. They'd seen a whole skeleton of some poor pit pony that had died down the mine. They'd seen a cave floor of shiny jet. It had sparkled like black diamonds in their lantern lights.

'We used to slide on this,' Dad had said, 'It's slippery as ice.' And he and Jay took off, sliding about in the flickering shadows on their own private underground skating rink, their laughter echoing down the mine's empty shafts and passages.

Jay didn't want to be down the mine. He didn't like the cold, the dark and the damp. Or the rats, whose glowing red eyes you saw as they scuttled past in the dark. But there was a part of him that didn't want this time with Dad to end.

‘Where we going today, Dad?’ asked Jay when they’d finished the tinned peaches.

‘This is the best yet,’ said Dad. ‘This place I’m taking you to is a massive cave. Hope I can still remember the way.’

They set off from the van, carrying lanterns.

‘You got some food supplies in that backpack?’ Dad asked Jay.

Jay nodded. ‘Cans of beans.’

Dad frowned. ‘We’re going have to go out for more food soon. Maybe back to the shipping container, like I said.’

‘I brought two torches,’ said Jay, mainly to stop Dad’s mind drifting from the shipping container to the Silver Bullet. ‘What did you use for light, when you explored down here with your mates?’

When they went far from the mine’s entrance on these expeditions, they always carried plenty of light. They didn’t want to be lost, in the dark, in the mine’s maze of tunnels.

‘Candles,’ said Dad. ‘Once, the air was so bad they went out. We had to feel our way back along the walls to the main tunnel. I was totally freaked out! I kept hearing noises and thinking ghosts were coming to get me.’

They turned down a side tunnel. This looked like an even older part of the mine. Some wooden posts were crumbling, eaten away by creeping white fungus. Fungus, unlike Verdans, didn’t need light to survive.

The sound of trickling water was growing louder. Dad tilted his head upwards, as if he could see to the surface.

'There's a lot of water coming down. It must be raining hard up there.'

The next passage was the narrowest they'd been down so far, just a slit in the rock. They had to go down it single file, Jay's knuckles brushing the slimy walls.

'This wasn't dug out by miners,' said Dad. 'It's part of an underground cave system.'

Jay wound up his lantern to give extra light. Its rays hardly penetrated the dark.

Dad said, 'It's not far now.' Then he stopped and said, 'Listen.'

Jay listened. He'd become used to the constant drip and trickle of water in the mine. But this was different. It was as if the rocks around them were coming alive, playing their own weird music. There were high piping notes like flutes; low booming ones, as water was forced, under pressure, through cracks and fissures.

'Must be a terrific rain storm up above,' Dad said.

Jay realised there was water, foaming around his feet. He said, 'My trainers are wet.'

'I think we should go back,' Dad decided. 'You get flash floods in cave systems sometimes.'

Jay felt something brush his trainer.

'Dad, look!' Scuttling past their feet was a heaving sea of rats, tumbling over their shoes. Their eyes, where the lantern caught them, flashed like rubies. They were running *towards* the cave, escaping something.

Jay said, 'Which way do we go?'

'Back to the van,' said Dad. 'We don't want to get trapped down here.'

They turned around, hurrying as fast as they could, but soon they were wading through swirling water.

'There's definitely flooding somewhere,' said Dad, his voice worried.

Now they were out of the narrow passage, back in the old mine workings.

'Listen,' said Dad again. They heard rocks shifting somewhere, grinding against each other. Then echoing through the mine came an ominous growling.

'Wait here,' said Dad. 'I'll just check what's ahead.'

'Dad!' Jay protested.

But Dad was gone, his lantern light swallowed by the dark. Jay stood in the darkness, shivering, listening to the water moving in the rocks all around him.

He held up his lantern to see if Dad was coming back, and for a second he thought his eyes were playing tricks. There was a water surge coming from up ahead. Foamy waves were boiling along the tunnel towards him, glinting black in the lantern light.

'Dad!' yelled Jay.

For a second he stood, frozen: not wanting to turn and run; knowing the way forward was blocked. He saw the waves snap one of the roof supports like a matchstick.

He turned and, splashing and slipping in a blind panic,

stumbled back towards the cave. Water chased behind him. He heard timber groaning and cracking, rocks crashing down as roof tunnels caved in. And all the time, *Dad, Dad* was sobbing through his mind.

Jay burst into a huge space. Water foamed past him but then slowed to a trickle. The main torrent hadn't followed him here. It had drained down a shaft somewhere, to another level of the mine.

Panting and terrified, Jay held up his lantern. The cave was as vast as a cathedral. Its walls glittered with black jet. Giant limestone blocks lay tumbled all around, piled in soaring slopes against the walls.

He heard movement, a sort of shuffling sound. Then a voice, barely more than a whisper, begged, 'Let me see the light.'

Jay swung wildly round. 'Gran!' he cried. 'What are you doing down here?'

CHAPTER 8

If Jay thought Gran would be pleased to see him, he was wrong.

She squinted at him in the gloom. Then both green hands flew to her mouth in horror. She backed off, stumbling out of the light.

'There's an Immune down here!' she shrieked.

Jay shone the light on her panic-stricken face. 'Gran, don't be scared,' he said, shocked by the fear in her eyes. 'It's only me, Jay. I won't hurt you.'

'Keep away from me!' shrieked Gran. 'It's because of you I'm being punished!'

Jay stared at her. 'What are you talking about?'

'I was arrested as an Immune Sympathiser.'

'But I haven't seen you in ages! And I'm your grandson!' said Jay, bewildered. 'That's not a crime, is it?'

'We must keep away from Immunes,' droned Gran, as if she was reciting something she'd learned. 'We mustn't help or support them in any way. No contact is acceptable. The punishment is Etiolation.'

She crept nearer the light, with a look of desperate longing on her face.

'I don't understand,' said Jay. 'Etiolation, what's that?'

He'd heard the word before, or something like it. But he couldn't recall where.

'We get put in the dark,' Gran moaned. 'We don't like the dark.'

Jay closed his eyes, breathed deeply, tried to quiet his jabbering brain. 'How did you get into this cave?' he asked.

'The Cultivars put me in here,' said Gran. 'I must be punished.'

'Yeah, yeah,' said Jay. '*How* did they put you in?'

'Up there,' said Gran. She raised her eyes to look into the dark. Jay held up the lantern.

'Don't take the light away!' begged Gran.

Jay put the lantern down on the rock. 'It's all right, Gran,' he soothed her. 'It's all right, you can keep the light.'

He shrugged off his backpack, got out a torch and shone it up into the cave roof. A great pile of stone blocks were piled up to the roof, like a magnificent ruined staircase. And right at the top, there was a trapdoor. Hope sparked in his swirling brain.

'Is that the way they put you in, through that door?' Jay asked Gran, excitedly. 'We can just climb out that way, go and find Dad! We can't go back the way I came, the tunnels are flooded, the roof's caved in. I lost Dad. I have to find my way back to the mine entrance – '

'We're being punished,' Gran interrupted. 'We're Immune Sympathisers. We must stay here.'

She seemed less distressed now she was crouching by the lantern. She began to lick water from the cave wall with her green, furry tongue.

'We?' said Jay. 'Are there other people in here with you?' He swung his torch around the cave, round the tumbled blocks and stalagmites, like giant melted wax candles.

There were Verdans everywhere, lots of them, staggering zombie-like from all corners of the cave, towards the light.

'What's happened to them?' gasped Jay.

And then he remembered the sick plant in Gran's garden, the one she found under the plastic bucket, deprived of light.

These Verdans had the same symptoms. Their chlorophyll skin, even their eyes, had turned deathly yellow. Their limbs were long and spidery thin. Some were so weak, they could barely walk. Their bones seemed to have turned to jelly, their legs wobbled and they couldn't hold their necks up. Their heads flopped onto their chests like drooping flowers.

Those who couldn't walk slithered towards the light. They dragged themselves over rocks like giant yellow worms. Those who'd been in the dark the longest had fuzzy white fungus attacking their bodies and faces, the same fungus that was rotting away the mine's wooden roof supports.

Jay backed away, horrified. But they were harmless, too weak to hurt him, even if they'd wanted to.

Then he recognised two of them. They were Viridian's parents. The last time he'd seen them, they'd been drinking rain water at the Diner.

'What are *they* doing here?' Jay asked Gran. 'Why are they being punished?'

But Gran didn't answer that. Instead she looked up towards the trap door. 'Guards!' she shrieked. 'There's an Immune down here!'

Jay stared upwards, new alarm on his face. 'Are there guards out there? Are they Cultivars?'

'Guards!' Gran was still shouting. 'Come and arrest him!' But her cries were too feeble for anyone to hear outside this cave prison.

'Shhh, stop it!' said Jay. He couldn't believe Gran would betray him. 'I'll get you out of here,' he said.

'No,' said Gran cowering. 'Don't touch me. You're a filthy Polluter. You're an Immune. All Immunes are enemies.'

'Gran!' said Jay frantically. 'If you stay here, you'll end up like this lot. It's horrible. Just look at them!'

'I must be punished,' said Gran, almost smugly. 'My sentence is ten days' Etiolation.'

'For heaven's sake, Gran!' cried Jay. 'Why are you talking like that? Like you *deserve* it? You haven't done anything wrong.' He grabbed her wrist and dragged her, weakly protesting, behind him. None of the Verdans tried to stop him. They were all too busy jostling to get some light on their sick, etiolated bodies.

To try and make her move faster Jay said, 'We're going up to the light, Gran. You'll have all the sunshine you want,' even though he guessed it was still raining on the surface.

What if there were Cultivars up there too, to stop the prisoners escaping? Jay couldn't think yet how to deal with them. One thing at a time. He played his torch over the tumbled limestone blocks piled crazily, one on top of another. They had to climb those to reach the trapdoor.

It looked perilous. But if the prisoners had come down that way, there had to be a way up.

Jay's foot hit something soft. He shone his torch downwards.

'*Eurgh!*'

He sprang back, sour bile rising in his throat. There was a Verdan down there. But unlike the others, she was chained to a rock. It looked like she'd been down here longer than the other prisoners. Her limbs were like soft yellow jelly: she couldn't lift them. The fungus from the mine had invaded her weakened body. Spores, like white dust, puffed out of her skin.

Disgust struggled with pity inside Jay's mind. 'Why's she chained up?' he asked Gran. 'Who is she?'

'She's an Immune Sympathiser. A traitor. Her punishment is death.'

'What?' said Jay. He couldn't believe what he was hearing. 'What's she done?'

'It must have been something bad,' said Gran.

Fighting revulsion, Jay knelt down. 'What's your name?'

The prisoner tried to lift her head. She couldn't. When she spoke, fungus spores came in clouds out of her mouth. Her voice was so feeble, Jay had to bend closer. She smelled like mouldy graveyards.

'Teal,' she whispered.

Her pale yellow eyes were glazed over. She was dying and Jay knew there was nothing he could do. Even if he could free her from her shackles, there was no way he could get her up to the surface.

He let go of Gran's wrist and got the other torch out of his backpack. He switched it on and placed it on the rock near her.

Teal turned her head towards it and it seemed, for a moment, to bring life back to her ravaged face. But it was only her eyes reflecting its beam.

Jay knew it wouldn't save her; it was sunlight Verdans needed. But it might comfort her, down here in the dark.

Jay got up. His whole body felt heavy, weighed down with despair.

Then he ordered himself, *Get moving. You've got to find Dad.*

Gran bent to pick up the torch. 'No, leave it for her,' said Jay angrily.

Teal's eyes were closed now. She wasn't moving at all. But he wasn't going to let Gran steal her light.

Jay grasped Gran's hand. She tried to pull away again.

'I'm not an Immune, right?' lied Jay, desperately. 'Soon as we get out of here, I'm going to get myself injected with the virus. So you're not in any trouble, Gran.'

'Will you tell the Cultivars?' said Gran. 'Will you tell them I'm not an Immune Sympathiser?'

'Course I will. I'll tell them as soon as we get out of here.'

Together they started the long climb up the limestone slope, with Jay's one remaining torch lighting the way.

Jay didn't look back. He forced the image of Teal out of his mind. It was one burden too many.

Instead, he asked, 'Gran, why do Verdans hate Immunes so much?' He was desperate to know. It was terrifying when Cultivars wanted to kill you and Verdans hated you and you didn't know why.

But Gran just repeated, 'All Immunes are enemies.'

Jay sighed, looked upwards. They didn't have far to go. He'd worried that Gran wouldn't make the climb. But, even Etiolated, she moved creepily fast. Springing from block to block like a green monkey, more agile than she'd ever been as a human.

Jay caught her up, just below the trapdoor.

Cautiously, he tried lifting the door. He'd already decided it was probably locked. So when it opened easily, it took him by surprise.

It was grey outside but daylight hurt his eyes after so long underground. His heart thumping, Jay gently lowered the trapdoor again, in case any guards saw.

'Keep quiet, Gran!' he hissed, a finger to his lips. He didn't want her shouting out to the guards, like she had before.

But he needn't have worried. Gran was lapping at a pool in the rock, lost in her own Verdan world, where only water, sunshine and nutrients mattered.

Gran hadn't felt any pity for the dying Teal. She didn't seem to care about finding Dad.

Jay slumped down on a rock to think. He had no idea what was waiting out there. He felt more alone than he'd ever done in his life.

He looked down into the dark cave, far below them. The lantern had gone out. He saw the torch he'd left for Teal, its white beam shining out like a star. But he knew the other prisoners would soon be slithering and staggering over to take her light for themselves, like Gran had tried to.

It hardly mattered, because Jay instinctively knew that Teal had died. She didn't need the light any more.

Jay suddenly had to get out. Not caring who saw, he flung the trapdoor wide open. He'd rather take his chances with the Cultivars than stay in this hellish prison.

He climbed out, blinking in the cloudy daylight, pulling Gran behind him. 'Get ready to run,' he said.

But there was nobody there.

He rubbed his eyes, stared round again. But he couldn't see a living soul, human, Verdan or Cultivar.

CHAPTER 9

Jay crouched with Gran in tall grass beside the trapdoor. He made a spy hole between the green stems.

'There's nobody here,' he whispered to Gran.

He wasn't in the scrubland anymore, with those strange, round hills. He seemed to be in some kind of industrial estate – there were several of them on the edges of Franklin. But the whole place looked derelict. Grass was growing in the car parks. The units had broken windows with green shoots of ivy sprouting through. A fork lift truck was rusting away.

Jay said to Gran, 'I thought you said there were guards. They left the trapdoor open. You could have escaped any time.'

'Escaped?' said Gran. She looked shocked and terrified at the very idea.

And Jay knew then why there were no guards, why the Cultivars could leave the door unlocked. The prisoners were so brainwashed and scared, they'd stay exactly where they were told.

'Didn't anyone even *try* to escape, Gran?' said Jay.

Gran shook her head.

So why was Teal chained to a rock? wondered Jay, then blocked all thoughts of Teal out of his mind. Dad was his priority.

He stood up. No Cultivar ran out of the abandoned buildings, yelling, 'Arrest the Immune!' But why should they? Viridian had told them, weeks ago, that Jay was dead. They weren't searching for him any more.

There must be other humans left in Franklin. Jay could just blend in with them. With any luck, no Cultivar would give him any trouble. And, if they did, he'd tell them, 'Back off! Me and Viridian are good mates. Blood brothers. He'll tell you so himself.'

Jay scanned the skyline, trying to get his bearings. It had stopped raining and the sun had slid out between grey clouds.

'We're going to get Dad now, Gran,' said Jay, without looking round.

An image flashed through Jay's mind, of Dad drowning in dark, swirling flood water. He crushed it, brutally. Instead he constructed another picture in his head. In this one, Dad was alive. He'd escaped the flood and he was sitting in the van, scoffing sardines. When Jay turned up he'd grin and say, 'Took your time, didn't you?'

But Jay had no idea how to get to the mine entrance from here. He wasn't even sure where he was now. Dad and he must have walked several kilometres underground to get to the cave.

Then, staring over the low buildings on the industrial estate, Jay saw the two Gothic towers of the Victorian town hall rising over the trees. That was in the centre of Franklin, in the market square. If he headed for those two towers he could head out again to the plot by the motorway where the Diner had been. From there he was fairly certain he could retrace the route Dad had driven to the mine entrance.

It would be a long hike. He'd need supplies from the shipping container. Dad had been pretty sure that would have survived the blast.

'You ready, Gran?' said Jay, and turned round.

Gran wasn't there.

For one horrible second, he thought she'd climbed back down into the cave to serve her prison sentence. But then he saw her, in a wilderness of plants, soaking up the autumn sun. She looked totally at home, almost lost in brambles, blackberry juice smearing her green skin, part of the plant world now, not Jay's.

Jay persisted: 'You coming with me to find Dad?'

Gran opened her green, glowing eyes. She said, 'I want to stay here.'

Jay didn't know whether to be sad or angry. He said, 'Well, *I'm* going. When I find Dad, we'll come back for you, right?'

Gran didn't even answer. She closed her eyes again and lifted her face to the sun's watery rays, alien, unreachable.

Jay started off. He hadn't wanted to leave Gran behind.

But part of him was relieved. For the first time in his life, he didn't trust her.

'She's not Gran anymore,' he told himself. 'She's a Verdan. She'll betray you.'

It felt like a person he loved had been taken from him, forever.

Jay had only taken a few steps, when another thought hit him. He rushed back to the trap door and called into the dark, 'The door's open. You can just climb out of there!'

He looked down. He couldn't see Teal's torch beam any more. But there was a weak shaft of light from the open trap door that slanted down to the cave floor. Jay could see some prisoners standing in the patch of light, their blank faces staring up.

'You can be free!' Jay called to them. But they didn't seem to understand what he was saying.

Sighing, Jay started off again. At least one question was settled. If he had the choice, which he didn't, he wouldn't want to be Verdan. And definitely not a Cultivar. Not after he'd seen how they treated their prisoners.

He headed for the town hall towers. He didn't see any need to hide – an Immune didn't look different from any other human. But, at the same time, it'd be stupid to draw attention to himself. So when he got to a housing estate he kept a low profile, sneaked down back alleys full of wheelie bins. Accidentally he turned into a main street. He was about to duck back when he realized that there was no-one here.

The estate was like a ghost town. Every house seemed abandoned. Every garden was a wasteland of withered weeds.

Where is everyone? Jay thought.

Doors and windows were wide open. And, wherever the people were, they hadn't gone by car. There were cars everywhere, in driveways, on the streets, even in the middle of the road. Jay peered into the open door of a four-wheel drive. Moss was growing on the seats, grass sprouting from the carpets. Bright green algae had invaded all the window and door seals.

Jay wandered into a house, through the open door. 'Hello!' he yelled. 'Anybody home?' His voice echoed eerily through the silent house. No-one replied.

Everything had just been left, as if Verdans had no use for all their previous possessions. There was an open laptop, its screen covered in dust. Jay tried to power it up. The screen stayed grey and lifeless.

He tried switching on the television, then the light – there was no electricity. He picked up their home phone. The line was dead. He turned on the taps. Dry gravel trickled out.

He wandered back into the living room, and wrote his name on a gritty table top, just to reassure himself he still existed.

He picked up a grey hoodie, thrown over a chair. It didn't feel like stealing; Verdans didn't need this stuff any more. It was far too big for him. But that was good. Jay tugged the hood over his face, let the sleeves dangle over his hands to hide his skin colour.

He probably didn't need to do this. Just being human wasn't a crime, was it? But somehow, he felt better disguised.

Jay tramped upstairs. Maybe there was something else he could use. He found a mobile and tried to turn it on, but it was dead too. Jay threw it back on the bed in disgust.

His guts clenched in panic at a sudden sound in all this deathly silence. A sort of whining noise, from downstairs. Cautiously Jay crept to the top of the stairs, looked down. A scruffy little dog was standing in the open front door.

'Hey, boy!' said Jay, relieved. He went clattering down, pleased to find another creature that hadn't got the virus.

Jay sat down on the doorstep, scratched the small, scrawny terrier behind its ears.

'Hey, boy,' said Jay again, as the dog whined and licked his hands. 'Did you live in this house?'

He'd probably been the family pet. But now his fur was matted and tangled with sticky burrs and twigs. It looked like the Verdans had walked away from their pets as well. It didn't take a genius to work out why.

'You're an animal, a Polluter like me,' said Jay. And, in the new Paradise on Earth, there was no room for dirty Polluters.

Jay told the dog, 'You can come with me if you like. I'm off to find Dad. Then there'll be three Polluters together. Us against the world!'

He stroked the fur on the dog's head. It lunged and bit him. Snarling savagely, it clung on, trying to take a piece out of his hand.

'Hey!' shouted Jay, in shock and pain, trying to wrestle his hand free. But the family pet had gone feral, forced to hunt for food. And humans were just bigger, meatier prey.

Jay grabbed the dog's collar with his free hand, twisting it tight. The dog had to open its mouth to breathe and Jay snatched his hand away.

He leapt up, looked round for a weapon in case the dog attacked again. He grabbed a stone garden gnome from beside the doorstep and raised it high above his head like a club. For a few seconds Jay and the dog snarled at each other like two wild beasts. Then the dog whimpered and slunk away into the bushes.

Panting, Jay found himself alone, holding a garden gnome high above his head. Suddenly embarrassed, even though there was no-one to see, he put the gnome carefully back beside the doorstep.

He looked at his hand and swore. Blood was trickling from two puncture wounds in the soft flesh between his thumb and first finger.

Red blood would give him away as human immediately. There was plenty of water around after the recent torrential rain, so Jay washed his hand in an overflowing bird bath. He went back into the kitchen and, wincing, wrapped up his injured hand in a tea towel.

He looked in the kitchen cupboards for food but there was nothing. So he ripped open a can of beans from his backpack and wolfed down the contents. He'd get more from the shipping container.

He checked himself in the hall mirror, made sure the hoodie top hid his face and the long sleeves his hands. Then he went out again onto those spooky, empty streets, heading towards Franklin town centre.

Jay took a short cut through an old graveyard. It seemed perfect for Verdans, with all its neglected corners choked with stinging nettles and huge willow trees shedding dead leaves in yellow drifts all over the tombs. But the graveyard, like everywhere else, was deserted.

Maybe the Verdans have moved out of town, to the countryside, thought Jay. *Maybe they're living in the woods and forests now.*

But he couldn't think where the humans had gone.

He turned left down an alley and emerged in the High Street. At last, he knew where he was. He was sure he'd see Verdans sitting at tables outside the Mineral Café, and maybe a few humans scattered around.

But there was no-one in the main street either. No-one sitting at the Mineral Café's tables sipping nutrient smoothies. The Café had a 'Closed' sign on its door.

Jay felt like the guy in a horror film who wakes from a coma and finds he's the only survivor in a creepily empty town where the road and buildings are crumbling and everything is gradually returning to wilderness.

Then he heard a growling of engines. He shrank back into the doorway of the Mineral Café. Three black armoured Humvees sped past in convoy, the first one flying a green flag on the bonnet. The convoy made a left turn, into a cobbled lane that led into the main square.

That was the way Jay was going. Before he reached the end of the cobbled lane Jay could see a sea of bobbing green heads. When he turned into the square, he murmured, 'So this is where they all are.'

Every Verdan in Franklin seemed to be assembled here, in front of the town hall. Jay couldn't see any humans at all.

He thought: *Surely I can't be the only one left?*

Jay ducked back into the street he'd come down. He'd totally underestimated the Verdan takeover. Now even his hoodie didn't make him feel safe. It concealed his skin colour, the red-stained towel. But he still looked different. Verdans never covered their heads; they liked to soak up as much light as possible.

Jay peeped cautiously out to see what was going on. What were the crowd waiting for? They didn't seem excited or joyous. They were meekly standing there, quiet and obedient.

Then he saw the taller, darker green Verdans, some standing like soldiers around the edge of the square, some moving among the crowd.

'Cultivars,' whispered Jay to himself. Now he knew why the Verdans were so subdued.

They're scared, thought Jay.

He saw a Cultivar, pushing his way through the crowd. The Cultivar pounced on a Verdan man and began to drag him off. The nearest Verdans stared at the ground, as if it was none of their business. The Verdan didn't struggle. His head drooping, his feet shuffling, he let himself be led away.

Suddenly, loud military music blasted out into the square. The Verdans all seemed to be gazing in one direction, at a stone balcony, on the first floor of the town hall.

The music stopped. A voice boomed out into the square. 'Verdans, welcome Franklin's Cultivar Commander.'

More and more Cultivars pushed through the crowd, very alert, towering above the ordinary Verdans, their green eyes flickering everywhere.

Viridian walked out onto the balcony, and the Verdans started shouting and cheering as if their lives depended upon it.

He was only just recognisable as the teenage boy Jay had met, that day at the Diner. He wore simple, loose, karate trousers. He was bare-footed, bare-chested. He was much taller, bulkier than before, his muscles more pumped up and sinewy. His veins stood out like creepers, writhing under his skin, carrying green sap around his body. His skin was so dark green it was almost purple.

He'd shaved his head and instead of hair, a Mohican crest of vicious, curved thorns ran from front to back over his skull and down along his spine.

You couldn't tell he'd ever been human. He looked like some fearsome alien warlord who'd come with his mutant warriors to conquer the Earth.

'He's a monster,' breathed Jay. But he was also mesmerizing. You couldn't take your eyes off him. His giant's body seemed to glow with a fierce, burning energy that might have come from the sun itself.

'Viridian! Viridian!' the Verdans chanted, as the Cultivars moved among them, seeking out those who didn't show enough enthusiasm, marching them away.

Viridian raised a mighty arm, snaked round with writhing veins. The Verdans immediately fell silent.

'Verdans,' began Viridian. Even his voice seemed to have changed. It was deeper, sinister, more cruel.

'I have called this rally,' he told the crowd, 'to warn you again about a threat to our very existence. The threat comes from Immunes. Seek out Immunes!' howled Viridian, his voice exploding in fury. 'They are terrorists. They want to destroy us!'

'Seek out Immunes,' the Verdans chanted back.

Viridian raised a clenched fist for silence. His eyes blazed at the crowd below.

'Do you know where an Immune is hiding?' hissed Viridian, his voice dark with menace. 'Do you know any Immune Sympathisers? If so, it is your duty to report them. I have imprisoned my own parents for their past friendship with an Immune. They are being punished as I speak. Even

Cultivars can't escape justice! There was a terrorist spy among us, I discovered – a high-ranking Cultivar! She was condemned to death by Etiolation! Even now, she is paying the ultimate price!'

Viridian's voice raved on. But Jay's mind was in turmoil. Viridian had betrayed his own parents, condemned a high-ranking Cultivar to death. Jay felt sure it was Teal he was talking about.

But he saved our lives, Jay was agonizing. *Mine and Dad's. If it wasn't for him, the Cultivars would have killed us. He said me and him were blood brothers.*

'You must be vigilant!' Viridian was shrieking like a madman at the crowd below, green spit flying from his mouth. 'The Verdan standing next to you might be a spy! Inform on anyone you suspect. Immunes and their spies and sympathisers, you have no place to hide. My elite squad of Immune Hunters will track you down, wherever you are!'

A squad of six Cultivars came marching out onto the balcony. They looked different to the others. Their chlorophyll skin seemed to have sprouted into strange, green, plant-like structures.

Then two more Cultivars came out. Jay stared at the human prisoner stumbling between them.

'Dad!' he gasped.

CHAPTER 10

The Cultivars shoved Dad to the front of the balcony, displaying their prisoner to the crowd below.

'This is the father of an Immune,' Viridian explained to the crowd. Viridian's frothing rage had disappeared. Now he was eerily calm, which, somehow, made him seem even more terrifying.

'Kill the prisoner!' the Cultivars screamed from the square, their eyes blazing.

'Kill! Kill him!' The Verdans obediently took up the chant.

Viridian raised his fist for silence.

'We shall kill him after he tells us where the Immune is hiding. We shall take him to the Research Station. He will talk then.'

That was when Jay totally lost control. He barged his way to the front of the crowd. The Verdans parted, sheep-like, to let him through. The Cultivars were gazing up to the balcony, watching their Commander's every move.

Now Jay was right below the balcony. He threw back his hood so Viridian could see him.

A Cultivar yelled from the edge of the crowd. 'It's the Immune!'

Jay's head whipped round in horror. The Cultivar who'd shouted was Thorn, who'd once been Jay's human friend Mac.

'Arrest him!' shrieked Thorn.

Jay screamed up to Viridian, 'Let my dad go!' Desperately, he pulled up his sleeve to show the towel, soaked with red blood. 'I'm your blood brother. You said so! Please, let my dad go!'

Viridian leaned over the balcony to look at him. Short, hooked prickles grew thickly across his chest and shoulders, as if he had his own personal body armour.

Jay stared into those hypnotic green eyes. Then he saw Viridian's thin lips twist into a ruthless smile. And he knew he'd made a dreadful mistake thinking this grotesque, power-mad monster would help him.

Viridian turned to his squad of Immune Hunters. 'Kill the terrorist,' he said. Then he turned and strode off the balcony.

'Jay!' Dad yelled down. 'Run!'

There was red shrieking panic in Jay's mind. He didn't know what to do.

'Run!' Dad screamed frantically, as his two Cultivar guards dragged him away.

Jay stared wildly around him. But the Verdans didn't touch him. Even the Cultivars hung back. They were leaving him to the Immune Hunters.

By the time the Immune Hunters came marching out of the town hall's main entrance, Jay was gone.

The Immune Hunters fanned out to search for him, moving fast on springy bare feet. Scientists at the Agricultural Research Station were trying to create Super Verdans, to take plant/human hybrids to new levels. And the Immune Hunters were the results of their latest experiments. Plant-like structures had grown on their chlorophyll skin: stinging spines, poison prickles, strangling tendrils.

A gap opened up in the crowd. An Immune Hunter got a sudden glimpse of a shock of dirty blond hair, as Jay swerved, in a crouching run, between Verdans.

The Hunter had leafy tendrils sprouting from her nose and ears and a thin creeper growing from her wrist, wound around it like fishing line around a reel, elastic, and strong as steel cable.

It shot through the air towards Jay. Its whippy end waved frantically, seeking something to cling to. It had minute sticky pads on the underneath, to help it fasten on and suck nutrients from whatever plant it attached to.

The Immune Hunter had been aiming the tendril at Jay's neck. She meant it to wrap round and round, tighten and choke the life out of him. But the creeper missed by centimetres, twined three times round the strap of Jay's backpack and immediately began to tighten.

Jay felt something tug at his right shoulder. He wrenched his head round, and saw the creeper, its questing end writhing towards his neck, and the Immune Hunter at the other end of the long, whippy tendril, her green teeth bared in a snarling grin, tiny shoots growing from her gums and writhing out of the corners of her mouth.

Then Jay was snatched violently backwards as the Immune Hunter reeled him in like a hooked, gasping fish. He tore his backpack off his left shoulder. As he staggered backwards, desperately struggling out of the right strap, he saw the creeper suddenly change direction, as if it had scented blood. It tried to loop around his wrist and burrow under the towel.

Jay dumped the backpack on the ground and took off. The creeper unwound from the backpack and came snaking after Jay's ankles.

And it almost got him. But there was a sudden commotion on the other side of the square.

'Get out of my way!' Thorn was shouting, shoving Verdans viciously aside, as he plunged into the crowd. Verdans surged here, there, frantic to obey the Cultivar's commands, but not knowing where to go. 'I'll arrest you all, you bunch of gutless cabbages!' he howled.

Panic spread across the square. The Immune Hunter lost sight of Jay in the jostling crowd. There was a shriek as the creeper clamped itself around a Verdan girl's bare leg and started burrowing to tap a vein.

In the mayhem, Jay ran from the square and plunged into the maze of cobbled alleys that was part of old Franklin.

The Immune Hunter reeled in her creeper. It coiled tightly again round her wrist. The nutrients it had sucked from the Verdan girl's leg were already coursing into the Immune Hunter's body. She stared into Jay's backpack.

'It's empty,' she said.

'I bet he's looking for human food,' said the Immune Hunter who'd just joined her. 'Viridian said to keep an eye on the shipping container, to see if he stocks up there.'

The first Immune Hunter nodded. 'Excellent idea. We'll set up a watch.' She added, 'I would have caught the Immune but for Thorn. That new recruit doesn't know his place. He could be a threat in the future.'

'Hmm,' said the other Immune Hunter. 'Didn't Thorn know the Immune before, when they were both human?'

The first Hunter caught on straightaway. 'I shouldn't be surprised if Thorn's an Immune Sympathiser, would you?'

'No,' said the second Immune Hunter, his green eyes flashing with cunning and malice. 'That wouldn't surprise me at all. I think Viridian should be told about him immediately.'

* * *

Jay finally stopped running. His head was swimming. He forced air into his burning lungs, panting like a dog.

He dived behind a big gorse bush, scattered with yellow flowers. Opposite him, behind its screen of trees, was the

Agricultural Research Station, the Cultivars' HQ, the place where Viridian had said they were taking Dad. Its three huge glass eco-domes flashed in the autumn sun.

Jay guessed that the Humvees would soon drive back from the town hall. One would have Dad inside. They'd have to stop at the entrance barrier. He had wild ideas of dashing up when they did and somehow setting Dad free. It was a crazy, desperate plan. But it was the only plan he'd got.

Jay peered over the bush. There were no Verdans about. And he seemed to have shaken off the Immune Hunters. He collapsed back on the ground. In these silent streets he'd hear the Humvees coming a mile away.

He breathed in deeply again, trying to stop his body shaking, and settled down to wait.

The flowers on the gorse bush smelled like coconut. Jay was reminded of Bounty bars. Gran used to slip one in his schoolbag every day, for him to eat at break time. He used to protest, 'Gran, I'm not a little kid any more.' But he wouldn't protest if she did that now. He wanted the old Gran back.

Jay's school was closed now too. He'd just cut across the jungly football field at Franklin High, running low through the long grass, and the school buildings were empty. Obviously Verdan kids didn't attend school.

Jay heard the snarl of engines in the distance: the Humvee convoy coming back from the square. Jay figured that the first one, flying the green flag, would have Viridian inside. Maybe Dad would be in the last one.

The Humvees sped past his hiding place.

His heart hammering, with no idea of what he was going to do, but desperate to do something, Jay got ready to break cover.

'Don't even *think* about it,' said a voice as a hand clutched his arm.

CHAPTER 11

It was a girl. Her skin was pink and her hair and eyes were brown. She was human.

Jay hardly had time to take that in. He was struggling to drag his arm away, but her bony fingers were clenched tight.

'They've got my dad!' he whispered frantically.

The girl spoke fast, urgently. 'You go out there now, you've got no chance. Wait until dark. We'll help you rescue him.'

Jay tore his arm away. But the three Humvees had already gone into the Research Station.

He slumped back behind the bush. 'How am I going to rescue Dad now?' he said, his voice cracked with despair.

'Don't you *listen*?' said the girl. 'We'll come back for him. You, me and the other Immunes.'

For the first time, Jay focussed on her. She had very long, tangled hair and a thin, peaky face.

'You an Immune?' he asked her.

'*D'oh*, yeah,' said the girl, scornfully. 'We're the only humans left in Franklin now.'

'My dad isn't Verdan,' said Jay.

'He soon will be,' said the girl. 'They'll make him. Unless he's Immune?'

'I don't know if he is,' said Jay. He felt like his head was going to explode. 'I don't know why *I'm* Immune. I don't know why they want to kill me.'

'Because of your blood, stupid.'

Jay wasn't listening. He was lost in his own tortured thoughts. What were they doing to Dad in there?

'We've got to get him out,' he said.

'They won't do anything to him tonight,' said the girl. 'They mostly rest when it's dark because their energy levels are low.'

'What, even Cultivars?' asked Jay.

The girl hesitated. 'No-one's sure what Cultivars do. They change all the time. I'm Toni Moran, by the way.'

'Jay Rainbird. Did you say there are more Immunes somewhere?'

'Yes. We're in hiding.'

'Take me to them,' said Jay, leaping up.

'No!' said Toni pulling him back down. 'How have you survived this long? Wait until the sun goes down. If a Verdan sees us they'll tell the Cultivars.'

'But *you're* out in daylight,' said Jay.

'Yeah, well,' said Toni, with more than a hint of swagger. 'I know how to look after myself, don't I?'

Her confidence impressed Jay. Maybe it was best to wait,

like she said. And he had to face facts. He probably couldn't rescue Dad without back-up. He had no idea how to get into the Research Station, let alone what was waiting for him in there.

'So, soon as the sun goes down, you take me to these other Immunes? Then we all go and get Dad?'

'I said so, didn't I?' said Toni, turning away.

Jay felt as if he could breathe again. He was still worried sick. But now he had a plan.

'How long until the sun goes down?' he asked Toni.

'Maybe four hours.'

It seemed like forever to wait. But he made a superhuman effort to keep calm.

'How'd you find me?' he asked.

Toni flashed him a scornful look, as if that was a stupid question. 'I was watching the rally. I followed you from there.'

'Where were you?' said Jay, amazed. 'I thought I was the only human in that whole square.'

'I was up high,' said Toni. 'In an empty building. Why'd you run out into the square like that? What were you saying to Viridian?'

Jay didn't want to admit how deluded he'd been to think he and Viridian had some kind of bond. So he said, 'I was begging him to let Dad go.'

Toni said, 'Are you crazy? Don't you know anything about him? He never, ever shows any mercy. That's how he got to be Cultivar Commander. Where have you been all this time?'

'Down a mine,' said Jay.

At last he'd said something Toni approved of. 'Good place to hide,' she admitted. Then she told him, 'Before I take you to the other Immunes, I've got to collect some food.'

'What?' hissed Jay furiously. 'How long will that take?' He'd steeled himself to wait until the sun went down but not a second longer.

'I don't know. But that's what I came out for. I'm not going back without food.'

Jay saw the defiant tilt of her chin. He closed his eyes and took several deep breaths. 'What kind of food?'

'Berries and mushrooms and stuff,' said Toni. 'I sometimes catch rabbits.'

'But that'll take ages!'

'We used to go on raids,' Toni explained. 'That was really quick. We stole food from closed-down shops, mostly tins. But there's no tins left now.'

For the first time, Jay felt he knew more than she did. 'I know where there are hundreds of tins. If I take you there, do you *promise* to take me straight to the other Immunes?'

'I promise.'

'But we've got to go for the tins now,' said Jay.

'Now?' said Toni. 'It's too dangerous.'

'But you were out in daylight!'

'I told you, I can take care of myself,' said Toni.

Jay was suddenly angry at the implications of what she'd just said, like he'd be a risk, or she'd end up having to save his life or something. He really resented that, after all he'd been through, all he'd seen.

'We go *now*,' he said, with a steely glint in his eye. 'Or I'm not showing you where the food is.'

Toni sighed. 'OK,' she said. 'How far is this place?'

He took her through the wood. They could see some Verdans straggling back from the town square into the countryside. But they were no threat. They walked slowly, scared that a Cultivar might pounce on them.

There was no path through the wood anymore. It was choked by nettles. Tender plants had been suffocated by briars and spiny brambles. A tabby cat, gone feral, snarled at them from a thorn thicket like a fierce little tiger.

Jay and Toni threaded their way through the clasping, prickly plants.

'Careful,' warned Jay, automatically. 'Don't get scratched.'

'We're Immune, remember,' said Toni. She checked her arms. 'Anyway, I haven't been scratched.'

Jay said, 'Do you come out to get food often? I mean, alone?'

'Oh yeah,' said Toni breezily. 'My dad knows I can look after myself.'

'Is your dad an Immune too?' asked Jay.

'Yes, you'll meet him soon. He's a plant scientist.' She laughed when she saw the alarm on Jay's face. 'Don't worry, he's not making freaky plant mutants. My dad is one of the good guys.'

Then they were out in the fields, wading through long grass, still slippery and wet from the recent rain.

'What's that over there?' asked Jay.

On the horizon, plumes of thick black smoke were rising. Long red tongues of flame leapt up, licking the sky.

'They've lit the funeral pyres again,' said Toni.

Jay could smell an awful stench of burnt bones, carried by the wind across the fields. 'What funeral pyres?'

'It's cows,' said Toni. 'There's been a mass slaughter of all the cows around Franklin and now they're burning the bodies.'

'Why?'

'Viridian ordered it. He says all animals are dirty Polluters. He's started by getting rid of cows.'

'You mean, he wants to get rid of *all* animals on Earth? He wouldn't do that!'

'He's a psycho. He wants to go back to a time when plants ruled the world. And guess who's going to be top plant? Him!'

'But even Verdans wouldn't like a world without animals. People love animals!'

'Verdans aren't people,' Toni reminded Jay, whacking at the willowherb with a stick she'd found in the wood so that downy seeds rose in clouds. 'They don't think like humans do. Anyway, the Verdans do anything Viridian tells them. He's got them scared out of their little planty brains.'

'He scares me too,' admitted Jay, staring at the funeral pyres smoking, burning and stinking in the distance like the fires of hell.

CHAPTER 12

Jay and Toni climbed over the fence, into the plot by the motorway where the Diner had once been parked.

It was all overgrown now, and so eerily quiet, you could hear the birds sing. Living here, Jay had got used to the drone of traffic. It had even lulled him to sleep. But there was no traffic at all on the motorway now.

The shipping container had survived the blast. Jay was relieved to see it, scorched, but still standing. Already ivy was claiming it, snaky creepers curling up the sides. In places, Jay could still make out Sage's hate-filled message:

POLUTERS MUST DIE

Toni picked up a piece of twisted aluminium.

'What's this?' she asked Jay.

Jay said, 'Me and Dad had a business here, an American Diner. It got blown up when the Cultivars came to get us. We escaped, and hid down the mine.'

Toni's eyes widened. 'You escaped a Cultivar attack? How?'

'Er, luck,' said Jay, uncomfortably. 'That's where the tins are.' He pointed to the container.

'There's a pond over there,' said Toni.

'No, there isn't,' said Jay.

Then he saw water glinting in the light. He stared in surprise, then realised it was the huge crater, made when the Silver Bullet blew up. It must have been filled up by rain.

Toni was already running towards the container.

When Jay joined her she was stuffing tins excitedly into her backpack. It was like she'd discovered treasure. 'Dad and the others are going to be really pleased when I turn up with all this stuff,' she said.

Jay found a strong plastic sack and started putting things in it.

'Do you want cooking oil?' he asked Toni, pointing to two catering-size plastic bottles.

'Yeah! Great! And get those scissors. And that frying pan.'

Jay picked up the scissors. They were big cutting shears that could hack through metal.

'Just take as much as we can carry,' he said, testing the weight of his sack. 'We can come back.'

Toni took some tins out of her backpack, shrugged it onto her shoulders and sagged with the weight.

'Come on,' said Jay, grabbing his sack.

They staggered out of the container. Toni looked around, to get her bearings. 'This way.'

Jay plunged after her, through the undergrowth. She led them round the edge of the crater, full to the brim with rain. Weeds crowded its edges and trailed in the water.

Bubbles were fizzing to the surface in a steady stream, coming up from somewhere beneath. Toni stopped and stared at them.

'That's not oxygen, is it?' she asked. 'It could be just methane gas, from something rotting down there.'

Jay gazed into the depths. It was hard to see. Ripples and refracted light distorted everything. But there were the mangled remains of the Silver Bullet – and some other big, bulky shape.

Jay opened his mouth to say, 'What's that?'

Then suddenly, he found a hand clamped over his face. Toni's eyes were centimetres from his own. She looked petrified.

She jerked her head towards the water and mouthed words.

Immune Hunter.

She took her hand away from his mouth and made pawing motions with her hands, like they should tippy-toe quietly away.

But Jay couldn't help looking down again, into the water. The bulky shape resolved itself into a crouching figure. Then it raised its head. Triumphant eyes glowed up at them.

'He's seen us!' said Jay. 'Quick, run!'

'No use. He'll catch us. Give me the sack.'

'What?'

'Give me the sack!' she shrieked.

The water was breaking into waves, as if something was about to surface.

Frenziedly, Toni unscrewed the cooking oil bottle and began to pour it over the water surface. It spread out in a thick golden film, breaking up in the centre into rainbows.

'Pour the other bottle!' she yelled at Jay.

His mind a whirl of confusion and panic, Jay poured, watching the oil glug out and a grease slick slide over the water.

Toni hurled her empty bottle away, just as the Immune Hunter, like a guided missile, blasted up from the depths of the pond. His head came first, breaking the floating layer of oil. His green hands clawed at the crater's edges, to haul himself out.

'Run!' shrieked Toni. They blundered away, through the tangled plants.

But the Immune Hunter was out now, a hulking green monster, his hair dripping oil and water, his skin glistening with grease and oxygen bubbles. He broke into a sprint, loping easily over the briars and stinging nettles.

Toni was way behind Jay already, slowed down by her heavy backpack.

'Dump the food!' he yelled.

She struggled out of the backpack, but it was too late, the Immune Hunter would catch her…

Then he began to slow down. His legs seemed to be buckling. He staggered, recovered, stumbled a few more steps, then fell to his knees.

Toni raced to join Jay. They watched the Immune Hunter crash down on his face into the grass, arms and legs flailing.

'What's going on?' whispered Jay. 'Is he dying?'

'I don't know,' said Toni. 'But he's covered in oil, so he can't take in CO_2 through his skin and convert it into energy. That's why he's collapsed.'

'Have you tried this before?' said Jay, gobsmacked.

'No,' Toni admitted. 'But my dad said it might work. Like, *theoretically*. But it does work, doesn't it? I mean, he's not getting up.'

Hidden down in the grass, the Immune Hunter had just enough strength to rip off a green plastic glove that protected his right hand. The latest experiments at the Research Station involved surgically grafting bits of plants onto Cultivars. The scientists had very ambitious surgery in mind. But they'd started with something simple. This Immune Hunter had had hundreds of sticky hairs grafted into his palm. They were taken from a tropical plant whose hairy leaves had glue so strong that rats could get stuck to them. The more the rat struggled the more glue the plant produced. The rat usually died, of fear or exhaustion or suffocation, long before it starved to death.

The Immune Hunter lay still.

Toni crept a few steps closer to the fallen Cultivar.

‘What are you doing?’ said Jay, dismayed. He picked up the sack. ‘Let’s go, before he recovers. It’s not safe.’

‘It’s OK, he won’t recover until the oil gets cleaned off,’ said Toni. ‘If he ever recovers.’

‘Who cares? Let’s get out of here.’

‘I need to see if he’s dying, to tell Dad. It’s useful information.’

Toni peered over the long grass. The Immune Hunter’s body lay, unmoving, in a soggy, oil-soaked heap. His long, tree-trunk arms, glistening with grease, were stretched out in front of him, palms down. His dark green face was turned to one side. His eyes were closed, his green lashes dripping oil, like golden tears. Could he be dead?

Eagerly, Toni knelt down, not too near. She inspected the fallen monster. Was it really this easy to kill Cultivars?

‘It’s OK,’ she called back excitedly to Jay. ‘Dad works night and day to find ways to defeat these things. And all I used was cooking oil! Come and look.’

Suddenly the Cultivar’s eyes shot open and his hand lashed out at her.

Toni screamed in shock, tried to scramble to her feet. But her long hair was caught, stuck to his palm by powerful glue. The Immune Hunter was squirming forward on his belly, his toenails leaving long scratches in the dirt. His blazing eyes fixed on her like a wolf’s on its prey. His other arm tried to grab her, but she twisted out of his way. Then he collapsed, his last strength gone.

Jay came crashing through the grass. Toni was screaming and struggling, trying to free herself from the Immune Hunter's hand. The glue from the sticky hairs on his palm was matting her hair into stiff clumps.

'Get me free! Get me free!' she was shrieking.

Jay threw himself on his knees, tried to tear her hair off the Cultivar's palm. 'I don't want to hurt you,' he said.

'It doesn't matter!' shrieked Toni. 'Just get me free!'

But the more Jay pulled, the more glue seemed to ooze out, setting her hair like concrete. He realized he'd get stuck himself, and snatched his hand back.

'Look!' screamed Toni. Jay twisted round, and saw another hulking green figure marching across from the Research Station.

'Use the scissors,' Toni begged.

Jay tipped Dad's scissors out of his sack. For one mad moment he thought she meant him to cut off the Immune Hunter's hand.

'I need a knife...' he started to say.

'Cut my hair!' Toni shrieked. 'Hurry up, the other one's coming!'

Clumsily, Jay started to chop off her long hair with the heavy shears. It was set so hard that he had to hack it really close to her head. When the last strand was cut, she leapt up.

Together they dived into the vegetation, burrowing deep into the bushes. They sat huddled together, Toni hugging her knees to stop them from shaking. Jay could hear the thudding of his own heart. He prayed the Immune Hunter couldn't hear it too.

They stayed there, listening. They heard deep menacing growls. They heard a grunt, branches snapping, heavy steps. Then nothing.

They stayed hidden, not daring to move or speak. Toni ran a hand over her hair, hacked close to her head in spiky clumps.

Jay gave her a brief, rueful grin.

To his surprise she grinned back, as if to say, with everything else going on, a bad haircut wasn't that big a deal.

Jay sat hunched up until he couldn't stand it a second longer. 'We can't stay here, we're wasting time.'

He scanned the plot. Both of the Immune Hunters were gone.

Toni's head popped up beside him. 'He must have recovered,' she said sounding crushed. 'The oil didn't work.'

'Or the other one took him away,' said Jay. 'At least you've got the food.'

He offered to carry the backpack, but Toni refused and trudged off, bent under the weight. Jay scooped his things back into his sack. He put Dad's shears into his hoodie pocket. They'd probably saved Toni's life. That would be a good story to share with Dad later, after Jay and the other Immunes had freed him from the Research Station.

Jay caught up with Toni, the heavy shears slapping against his ribs as he ran.

'Where are we going?' he asked.

'Not far,' she said. 'The science block, at Franklin High. That's where we Immunes are hiding.'

'Franklin High? You're kidding! It's right near the Research Station, the Cultivars' HQ. Viridian lives there.'

'Well, it's a good place to hide then, isn't it?' said Toni, plodding on. 'He's such an arrogant creep he'd never believe we were hiding right under his nose. And, anyway, the Research Station is where you need to be isn't it? To rescue your dad?'

CHAPTER 13

Jay crept through the waist-high grass on Franklin High's playing fields. He saw Toni's head pop up to check where they were. Patches of her pink scalp showed between clumps of hacked hair.

Down the road, the three glass domes of the Research Station flashed pink in the late afternoon sun.

So close. Yet so impossible to reach. The place would be swarming with Cultivars and Immune Hunters. And Viridian himself, freakish and monstrous, was somewhere in there, controlling it all.

The science block at Franklin High looked just as neglected and forgotten as the other buildings, with vines sprouting through broken windows and doors left wide open.

Jay caught up with Toni.

'I can't see anyone inside,' he whispered, wondering for a heart-stopping moment if Toni could be leading him into a trap. 'Where is everyone?'

Toni said, 'They're downstairs, in the basement.'

'How many of you are there?'

'Seven,' said Toni, 'including me and Dad. There used to be nine, but Ellie and Jake got killed by the Immune Hunters.'

'Killed?' said Jay, shocked. At the same time he was thinking, *Only seven?* He'd hoped there'd be loads of them, that they'd storm the Research Station in a heroic rescue.

'That's why we hide down there,' Toni was saying. 'Being underground all the time was driving me nuts. I had to get out, see some daylight.'

'Tell me about it.' Jay sympathised, remembering hiding out in the mine with Dad, like moles in the dark. 'Have you got any light down there?'

Toni's peaky face broke into a mischievous grin. 'We've got electricity,' she said.

'*Electricity?* How?'

'The Cultivars have a generator at the Research Station. We've diverted a bit of their supply.'

'Cool!' Jay said.

'We're trying to hack into their computer network, too.'

'The Cultivars have computers?'

'Oh yeah,' said Toni. 'Cultivars aren't just in Franklin, they're everywhere. Cultivars rule the world. Dad says their Commanders, like Viridian, are the new dictators.'

It was spooky, sneaking along silent corridors that, only a few months before, Jay had charged down with his mates. They felt full of ghosts. Old posters, torn and streaked white with pigeon droppings, flapped on notice boards.

'Did you go to school here?' asked Jay. He'd never noticed her if she had.

'Yes, did you?'

Jay said, 'I did once. Dad took me out.'

'Did he teach you at home?'

Jay laughed out loud. It was so long since he'd done that, the sound startled him. But it was just the idea of Dad, teaching lessons.

'No way,' he said. 'My dad's no teacher.'

Toni led him down a flight of steps. At the bottom was a door with a key pad beside it.

Toni keyed in some numbers.

'9955,' she told Jay. 'Remember that. It's OK, everyone, it's me,' she called out, pushing the door open. 'I've got food. And I've found another Immune.'

Toni tramped down some more stone steps, dumped her pack on the ground and rubbed her sore shoulders. Jay followed her, pushing his hood off. He made out a long, low room lit by a string of dimly glowing bulbs before a tall, stooped man came hurrying up. His gaunt face looked weary and harassed.

'Hello, Dad,' said Toni.

'What have you done to your hair? Where have you been?' Dr Moran fired questions at his daughter. 'You know the rules. No-one goes out without my permission.'

'I've got food,' said Toni. 'I went out to collect it. Someone's got to.'

Dr Moran ignored the food. 'Are you all right? You haven't been cut or scratched, have you?'

'No,' said Toni, surprised. 'Dad, I'm Immune!'

'You could still get tetanus,' said Dr Moran. 'We need to stay healthy.'

'Look, I'm all right,' said Toni. 'I just got sick of sitting around.'

'Well, that was stupid and selfish of you. What if you'd been caught? You know what they do to Immunes.'

'I wasn't caught!' said Toni.

Dr Moran glared at her. 'I've got more important things to do than worry about you.'

Toni scowled. Jay thought she was going to argue, but she didn't. 'I won't do it again,' she muttered.

Dr Moran's piercing blue eyes swung to Jay. 'So you're an Immune too?'

'Yes, he is,' said Toni. 'The Immune Hunters were after him. Go on, Jay, tell him.'

But Jay had other things to say. 'My dad's been taken prisoner – '

Dr Moran interrupted. 'Roll up your sleeve.'

'What?' said Jay.

'Roll up your sleeve. I want to see if you're what you say you are. And for that, I need some of your blood.'

Dr Moran produced a syringe. Jay winced as the needle was stabbed into his arm, just below his elbow. He watched the syringe fill with his dark red blood.

Dr Moran swabbed the skin puncture, then he was gone, hurrying into another room. He called back to Toni, 'Keep him there, until I've found out who he is.'

Jay looked at the small, stinging mark on his skin. 'What was that for?'

'The Cultivars have spies all over the place,' Toni explained. 'They could even recruit a human to infiltrate our group, pretending he's an Immune.'

Jay couldn't argue with that.

'Your blood group will show if you really are an Immune,' said Toni. 'Dad's checking it now. It won't take him long.'

'But what's my blood group got to do with it?' asked Jay, baffled.

'All of us Immunes are AB Rhesus negative. It's a really rare blood group. It makes us immune to the virus. My dad's been trying to find out why.'

She sat down, on the lowest stone step. 'We'd better wait here. You can't meet the others 'til you're cleared.'

Jay practically exploded. 'More waiting!' he shouted. 'You said we were going to rescue Dad! You said the others would help.'

He was horrified to see that Toni's face was full of doubt. 'You promised me they'd help,' he said again.

'I never actually promised,' said Toni quietly.

Jay howled out in frustration. 'I don't know what's going on! But if you won't help me, I'm going!'

He jumped up, but Toni grabbed his arm.

'You wouldn't stand a chance out there. Not alone.'

Jay hated to admit it, but he knew she was speaking the truth. He sat on the steps again, clenching his fists with tension until the knuckles were white as bone.

Dr Moran came back at last from the other room. 'It's OK,' he told Toni. 'He's Immune.'

Jay's mind was spinning with questions. But the most important one concerned Dad.

'Will my dad be Immune too?' he asked.

'Not necessarily,' said Dr Moran in that brisk, chilly way of his. 'Blood groups are very complicated. You could have inherited AB Rhesus negative blood from either parent, or neither. I've no time to explain and, frankly, you wouldn't understand if I did.'

Dr Moran strode away. Jay decided, *I don't like him.*

'My dad's got a lot on his mind,' Toni said apologetically. 'Come on. You can meet the others now.'

They followed Dr Moran to a room kitted out like a laboratory, with computers, microscopes, test tubes, centrifuges and all sorts of other equipment. The five other Immunes were sitting on lab benches, some looking through microscopes or staring at computer screens.

Jay's spirits rose. One was a child and one an old man. But the other three, two men and one woman, looked fit enough. That would make six of them along with Toni, Dr Moran and himself.

‘The Cultivars have got my dad,’ said Jay. ‘They’ve taken him to the Research Station. Toni said you’d help me rescue him.’

Dr Moran shot a look at Toni. ‘Well, I’m afraid she had no right to say that.’

‘Will you help me?’ pleaded Jay.

‘No,’ said Dr Moran.

Jay couldn’t believe what he was hearing. He appealed to the others. ‘I thought you were some kind of resistance group, freedom fighters!’

‘We are,’ said one.

‘But you’re all just sitting around!’ screamed Jay. ‘What happened to fighting back?’

‘We are fighting back,’ said Dr Moran. ‘We’re fighting the plant virus. We’re very, very close to a vaccine.’

‘But my dad needs help *now*!’ said Jay. ‘Toni, please!’

Toni said, ‘Dad, can’t we help?’

‘You know that’s not possible.’ Dr Moran turned to Jay again. ‘I’m sorry about your father. But if he’s an Immune, they’ll have already killed him. And if he’s not, they’ll infect him with the virus. And even if he was still alive and still human, we’re in a race to save the whole human species. One man’s life is of no account.’

Jay felt rage boiling inside him at the idea that his dad was of ‘no account’.

‘You sick, evil, cold-hearted creep!’ he yelled at Dr Moran. He whirled round to Toni. ‘You tricked me!’

‘I didn’t,’ protested Toni. She seemed almost as anguished as Jay. ‘I really thought we’d be able to help.’

‘You’re all pathetic cowards!’ Jay yelled at the Immunes.

The woman gave him a sad, kind smile. ‘We understand your distress,’ she said, ‘you poor child.’

Jay turned on her furiously. ‘I don’t give a toss if you *understand*. It’s help I need! Go to hell. I’m going to rescue Dad on my own.’

‘No, you’re not,’ said Dr Moran. ‘You’ve no idea what a powerful enemy we’re up against. Cultivars are a global power, not just in this little town.’

The two Immune men got up from their benches, moving towards Jay.

‘You have to join us,’ said Dr Moran. ‘Give your blood to help our research into a vaccine.’

‘Get off me!’ yelled Jay as the two Immunes took his arms. ‘You can’t keep me here!’

‘Dad,’ begged Toni. ‘Just let him go. Please.’

‘I can’t do that,’ said Dr Moran. ‘He knows where we’re hiding. He could tell the Cultivars.’

‘What?’ Jay shouted. ‘I hate them! I’m not going to tell them anything!’

‘You might not be able to help yourself,’ said Dr Moran. ‘We’re within days of finding a cure. Lock him in the boiler room.’

Jay was taken away, struggling, shouting and protesting.

CHAPTER 14

Jay hammered on the boiler room door and yelled to be let out. No-one came. When his voice was hoarse and his knuckles bleeding, he sat down on an upturned crate in the dim yellow glow of a single light bulb and looked around. Metal pipes snaked off in all directions. They'd once carried heat and hot water all around the science building. But they were cold now, unused.

The only door was bolted on the outside. There were no windows.

Jay's mood swung wildly between white-hot anger and black despair. The Immunes were supposed to be on his side. Instead they'd treated him like the enemy.

'When I get out, I'm going to kill them all. Then I'm going to kill those Cultivars,' Jay raged to himself, as tears of helplessness ran down his face.

The door opened and Toni came in, carrying food and drink. She closed the door behind her.

Jay smeared the tears off his face and called her an ugly name. 'Get away from me. You lied to me.'

Toni put the food and drink on the floor. 'Shut up and listen.'

Jay slumped down again on the crate. 'Say what you want. I'm not listening.'

'I didn't trick you,' said Toni. 'I really thought they might help. Look, I know you're angry. But... I'll come with you tonight to rescue your dad from the Research Station.'

'Oh yeah,' Jay said scornfully. 'That would be great! We'll wander in there, just the two of us, defeat the Cultivars and get Dad out. What planet are you on?'

'I know the layout of the Research Station,' said Toni.

'What?'

'My dad used to work there,' said Toni. 'I went there, loads of times. When the other scientists became Verdan, they started doing all these dodgy experiments trying to create the perfect plant/human hybrid. Dad resigned in protest.'

Jay didn't care about Dr Moran. 'Can you really get us into the Research Station?'

'Yeah, I think so,' said Toni. 'Provided the Cultivars haven't changed it too much.'

Jay stared into her eyes.

'You can trust me,' said Toni. 'I'm not lying to you. I didn't before either.'

Jay knew he'd got no choice. 'All right.'

'OK,' said Toni. 'But you're going to have to do what I say. First, we have to wait until dark to rescue your dad.'

Jay knew she was talking sense. 'OK.'

'And now,' said Toni, 'you have to tell my dad that you've changed your mind. That you realize he can't risk his mission to save the human race to rescue one man, even if he is your dad.'

'No way!' said Jay, glaring at her.

'If you don't, they won't let you out of this room. How are we going to rescue your dad then?'

Jay stared at her. 'Why do you want to go with me?' he asked her. 'You don't even know my dad. You've only just met me.'

'Because I'm sick of being here in this dump,' said Toni, her voice shaking with rage and frustration. 'I'm sick of having my blood taken, day after day. Dad says a vaccine is the best way to fight back. But I want to *do* something. I feel like a lab rat. I'm going crazy cooped up down here!'

Her eyes were blazing, her fists clenched at her sides. She seemed so intense, so full of passion, that Jay couldn't doubt her.

'OK,' he said. 'I'll do what you say.'

'Just make my dad believe it,' said Toni. 'And then, when it's dark outside, we'll sneak out of here. If your dad's in the Research Station, we'll find him.'

It wasn't too difficult. The Immunes were good people. They felt guilty about locking him up. Jay apologized. He said he knew he'd been selfish. That Dad might have to be sacrificed for the greater good.

The Immunes were very understanding. One said, 'We know it's awful. But the human race is facing its greatest crisis ever. We've all got hard choices.'

Another said, 'When we have a cure for the virus, your dad will be at the head of the queue.'

To spare Jay's feelings, they didn't add, 'If he's still alive.'

Dr Moran might have been more sceptical about Jay's sudden change of heart. But he was locked away, working on the vaccine, and couldn't be disturbed.

'He works all the time,' said one of the Immunes. 'He doesn't even seem to sleep. That man's a hero.'

Jay nodded in agreement, even though he still thought Toni's dad was a cold-hearted creep.

Toni told the other Immunes, 'I'll just show him around. OK?'

As he and Toni left the room together, Jay whispered, 'Think they suspected anything?'

'No, you did great.'

'When will it be dark outside?' Jay asked.

'It's dark already.'

'So why don't we go?' fretted Jay. 'What if your dad locks me up again?'

'He won't,' said Toni. 'He'll work all night, shut up in his room. But we can't get out of here until the others go to sleep.'

'*When* will they go to sleep?'

'Soon.'

'But what about my dad?' Jay started to argue.

Toni whirled round, her eyes blazing. 'Stop going on about your dad!' she snapped. 'Think you're the only one here who's lost someone? We've all had people we love go Verdan, or get killed. You know Ellie and Jake, who died? That woman you were rude to is Ellie's mum.'

Jay flushed. 'I didn't know,' he muttered. 'I'm sorry, I never thought...'

'Yeah, well, think now,' said Toni, stalking off.

* * *

Jay found her again, in a little cupboard-sized room next to the boiler room where he'd been imprisoned. He warned himself to shut up and hide his impatience. But Toni seemed to have calmed down. She was standing next to a tray of plants on a bench.

'They need more light,' said Toni. 'Some comes in daytime, through that ventilation grill. But it's not enough. And Dad won't give me a sun lamp for them. He says we can't waste electricity on non-essentials.'

'What are they?' asked Jay, trying to sound interested.

'Carnivorous plants,' Toni told him. 'I've got sundews, pitcher plants, Venus fly traps. But look.' She brushed a sooty spot off a leaf. 'They've caught this horrible fungus called black spot. It's the most deadly plant fungus there is. It spreads like mad. You can't stop it. It'll kill them, eventually.'

A shocking image slammed into Jay's mind. It was Teal, her skin covered in fuzzy white fungus, spores puffing from her mouth when she tried to speak. The image vanished in a split second, leaving him trembling.

'My absolute favourite is the Venus fly trap,' Toni was telling him. She pointed to a plant in a pot. It had leaves hinged in pairs like clam shells. Each leaf was the size of a penny and fringed with spikes. The leaves were green on the outside, and red as raw steak inside.

'You hungry?' Toni crooned to the Venus fly trap, as if it was a pet dog or cat. There was a lazy blue fly crawling along the bench. Toni's hand darted down. She pinched it between her thumb and finger, lifted it up and fed it to the fly trap. Instantly two leaves sprang shut around the fly, the spikes holding it in like prison bars.

'The leaves have got little trigger hairs on the inside,' said Toni. 'Soon as they feel prey moving, they snap the leaves shut. Clever, isn't it?'

Jay could hear the fly's buzzing whine coming from its leafy trap, see its legs sticking out between the spikes. Suddenly, he found himself paying attention. Repelled but fascinated, he peered closer at the struggling prisoner. 'Now what happens?' he asked Toni.

'The fly gets dissolved to soup. Really slowly. And the plant absorbs its nutrients. Yummy! Then when it's finished digesting, the trap opens again. And all that's left of the fly is its shell.'

'The plant eats it alive?' said Jay. 'That's disgusting.' He reached out a finger to trigger another trap.

'Don't do that,' warned Toni. 'If you trigger the traps too often, they die. It uses up all their energy.'

'How does this one work?' asked Jay, pointing to another plant. It had slender, trumpet-shaped traps, with little hinged lids on top.

'That's my pitcher plant,' said Toni. 'When a fly crawls in, the lid closes. Then the fly slips down into a pool of water...'

'Don't tell me,' said Jay. 'It gets dissolved to soup.'

'The plant drowns it first,' said Toni. 'Then dissolves it. Some pitcher plants are big. They catch rats.'

'Gross.' Jay shivered. 'Doesn't anything ever escape?'

'No,' said Toni. 'Once they're trapped, they're dead.' Then she reconsidered. 'Except wasps, sometimes. I've seen a wasp bite its way out of a pitcher plant, just munch through the walls and fly away.' Toni flapped her arms to show the wasp flying to freedom.

Jay frowned. 'Carnivorous plants are really creepy.'

'No, they're not,' Toni protested. 'They're amazing. They're top plant predators, awesome killing machines. My mum hated them, though, specially after she turned Verdan. She said plants shouldn't eat meat, they shouldn't catch and kill things...'

Jay stared at her, forgetting all about carnivorous plants.

‘Did you say your mum is a Verdan?’ he asked.

Toni nodded. ‘She wasn’t Immune like me and Dad.’

‘Did they force her to?’

Toni gave a bitter little smile. ‘No way. She bought into the whole Verdan thing. She was one of the first to get her virus shot.’

‘Did you want to get a virus shot too?’ asked Jay.

‘Yes,’ said Toni. ‘It would have been beautiful, if it had worked. Saving the planet, all Verdans living in peace with no wars...’ She looked embarrassed. ‘That sounds like a stupid dream now.’

‘No, it doesn’t,’ said Jay, fervently. ‘Don’t say that. I believed it, same as you. I tried to get a shot.’

‘I would have, but Dad took my blood for research and found out I was Immune. Then we had to go into hiding when the Cultivars started saying all Immunes must be killed.’

‘They’re the ones that spoiled it all!’ said Jay. ‘The Cultivars, the Immune Hunters. Viridian.’

‘My mum’s a Cultivar,’ whispered Toni.

‘What?’ said Jay.

‘When she turned Verdan, Dad took me to live with him. Mum wasn’t interested in me any more.’

‘My gran was the same,’ Jay burst out. ‘It was like I was a stranger.’

‘Then Mum moved to the Research Station, became a Cultivar. Dad said I mustn’t see her again. He said she’d betray us if she knew where we were.’

'She would have done,' Jay told her. 'She *definitely* would have done.'

Suddenly a dazzling light went on in his brain. 'Wait a minute! That's why you want to come to the Research Station, isn't it? It's not about rescuing my dad. It's about seeing your mum again.'

'I still want to help you get your dad back. Honest, I do. And I am sick of being down here. So I wasn't lying...'

Jay interrupted, more brutally than he meant to. 'Forget her! OK? She doesn't care. She's not your mum any more, she's a Cultivar. If she sees you, she'll tell the Immune Hunters.'

'I know,' Toni answered, in a small, quiet voice. 'But I still love her. I can't help it. I know I can't even let her see me. I just want to see *her*, from a distance. See she's all right.'

Jay sighed. He said, more gently, 'Getting food wasn't the reason you left the basement, was it? That was just an excuse. You went looking for your mum, didn't you?'

Toni nodded. 'I thought I'd see her at that big rally. All the Cultivars were there. But she wasn't. Why wasn't she there, when all the others were?'

'I don't know,' said Jay. He felt a sudden sick, chilly twist in his guts. 'Has your mum got a Cultivar name?'

'Yes,' said Toni. 'She chose it herself. It's Teal.'

CHAPTER 15

Jay's horror must have shown on his face, because Toni said, 'What's the matter?'

Jay knew he should tell Toni the truth, that her mum was dead. But he also knew he wasn't going to. If there was no hope of finding her mum in the Research Station, Toni might give up on the whole plan. And Jay needed her.

I'll tell her later, thought Jay guiltily.

Out of the blue, he said, 'My mum's dead.' He'd almost said, 'My mum's dead too,' but he stopped himself just in time.

Toni said, 'That's awful. Did the Immune Hunters kill her?'

Jay shook his head. 'She died years ago, in a motorbike accident. I never met her.'

'What, you mean, you don't remember her?'

'I never met her,' said Jay. 'She was pregnant with me when the bike crashed and she got fatal head injuries. I was born by Caesarean section, then they switched off her life support machine.'

Toni said, 'I don't know what to say.'

'You don't have to say anything,' said Jay. 'It was a long time ago.'

He didn't even know why he was bringing it up now. Yes, he did. It was to show Toni that he sympathised, that he knew what it was like to lose a mum, and that she would survive it.

Except, Toni didn't know that her mum was dead, because he hadn't told her.

Jay's nerves felt so raw and twitchy he couldn't stay still a second longer. 'Let's go,' he said. 'They must be asleep by now.'

Toni went ahead to check. She came back to Jay and whispered, 'OK.'

They crept past a door with a sliver of light showing underneath.

'My dad,' mouthed Toni. 'Working.'

They tiptoed through the lab to the basement exit and let themselves out into the dark world outside.

The night sky was beautiful. The sky over Franklin was clear, dark blue and crowded with stars. Without light pollution, they could see the constellations, and even shooting stars, whizzing across the sky with fiery tails.

While Toni stared upward, Jay ran ahead through Franklin High's overgrown playing fields towards the Research Station. All around was a deep, hushed stillness – no traffic sounds or police sirens or planes. Toni and Jay seemed like the only living creatures in the whole landscape.

Then Jay ran into some Verdans, hidden behind a bank of bindweed.

They were clustered in a tight little circle, like a mushroom fairy ring. Jay actually smashed into one. He bounced off and squirmed into the bindweed's tangle of twisted stems and big white trumpets.

'Watch out – Verdans!' he hissed as Toni ran up.

'It's OK, you can come out,' she told him.

Jay crawled out of his hiding place. The Verdans were still in their little circle, as if they were rooted there. Their green faces looked blank. Their wide-open eyes reflected silver in the moonlight. Jay snapped his fingers in front of one's face. There wasn't a flicker.

'It's like they're switched off,' said Jay.

'They're dormant,' said Toni. 'Verdans do that sometimes. They're conserving their energy, like plants do at night. When dawn comes, they'll wake up.'

'Do you think the Cultivars and Immune Hunters do this?' asked Jay. 'We could walk out with Dad and they won't even notice.'

'I don't know if the Cultivars go dormant,' frowned Toni. 'They don't behave like ordinary Verdans.' Then she added, 'You sure your dad is in there, by the way?'

'That's where Viridian said to take him. So that's where I'm looking.'

'And I'm looking for my mum,' said Toni. 'Be great, wouldn't it, if we both found what we were looking for?'

Jay didn't know how to answer that.

They left the little group of dormant Verdans and cut through the gardens of abandoned houses, heading for the Research Station.

'We can't go in from the front,' said Jay. 'There'll be security.'

'We'll climb the fence, round the back.'

Jay expected there to be sentries, patrolling the high wire fence. But there weren't. He wondered if it might be electrified, but when he hurled a rock there was no fizzing current, no shower of sparks. He couldn't see any CCTV either.

It was as if Viridian was inviting people to enter.

'Why is there no security?' asked Jay, uneasily.

'Because Viridian doesn't need it,' said Toni. 'The Verdans aren't going to rebel, are they?'

Jay nodded. That made sense. And it would be just like Viridian. So arrogant, so supremely confident that he couldn't imagine any challenge to his power.

Toni's gaze travelled up the fence. 'We've got to climb that.'

They clambered awkwardly up, using the mesh for footholds, handholds. The wire hurt, biting into their hands, leaving red weals.

When they were at the top the fence started to sway dangerously. Jay hurled himself over the top and went diving towards the ground. He crash-landed in soft grass on the other side. It knocked the breath out of him. He rolled over and lay on his back, stunned, staring dizzily up at the spinning stars.

Toni jumped down more carefully. They crept between trees, through quivering pools of moonlight and shadow, all the time watching out for guards.

Then suddenly, the trees stopped. The curved wall of the first dome was only metres away. It soared high above them, lost in darkness.

Toni ran over. Jay hissed, 'Be careful.' But she already had her nose pressed against one of the glass panes.

She waved him over. Crouching, he stared through the glass too. The darkness inside was dotted with red and green lights, some flashing. Here and there a blue computer screen glowed.

The Verdans were living like primeval plants. But the Cultivars seemed to have all sorts of sophisticated hi-tech equipment.

'So is this where we're going in?' he whispered. 'I can't see any Cultivars.'

Toni shook her head. 'It's too risky – there might be guards on night duty. This way.'

Jay didn't argue. She was the one who knew her way around here. He followed her to the second dome, which seemed full of huge green leaves.

'When Dad worked here, they used this dome to grow experimental plants,' whispered Toni. 'This is the best place to get in.'

‘But where d’you think my dad will be?’ asked Jay. Then he added quickly, ‘And your mum?’

‘In the third dome,’ said Toni. ‘That’s where the labs are and the offices and living quarters – and the prisons.’

She pushed aside some creeping vines and said, ‘Good. It’s still here.’ There was a concrete drain, like a deep open trough, coming out under the glass walls. Water, slimy with green algae, pooled in the bottom.

Toni slid into it, head first, and wriggled through into the dome. Jay waited anxiously. Then he heard her voice, echoing through the drain. ‘Are you coming or not?’

Jay lay down in the concrete trough, and pulled himself forward commando style. His head emerged almost immediately on the other side. He crawled out of the drain and stood up.

The dome smelled hot and damp and boggy. Moonlight, slanting in through the glass, washed over a jungle of giant plants.

‘They’re carnivorous,’ said Toni, in an awe-stricken voice. ‘But these are massive.’

Pitchers, more than two metres tall, rose in a sinister forest all around them. Some were white, like tall ghosts. Some were purple with swollen bases, like fat bellies. They had darker red veins running through them, like putrid meat. Clumps of bushy sundews, a metre across and waist-high, writhed their deep-red sticky tentacles.

‘Why are they all so big?’ whispered Jay.

‘Maybe growth hormone,’ said Toni, in a hushed, wondering voice. ‘Or genetic engineering? Look at the Venus fly traps.’

Their double-lobed traps were different sizes, some as big as tractor wheels. One, hanging just above Toni’s head, was tightly closed. Toni could see a bulge inside. It was digesting something.

She reached up a hand to stroke the trap. ‘What have you caught?’ she asked it.

A green head, with an armoured crest like a stegosaurus, rose above the carnivorous plants. Viridian fixed his glowing eyes on Jay.

‘I knew you’d come,’ said Viridian. ‘You humans are so weak, so sentimental.’

Without turning his head he rasped out a command. ‘Immune Hunters!’

Figures came sliding, springing out from the green jungle.

‘Run!’ Jay screamed at Toni. He started to move but didn’t have a chance. Viridian reached him in two strides, crashing through the carnivorous plants.

As he twisted in Viridian’s grasp, Jay thought Toni might escape. She was diving into the drain, already wriggling through. But the woman Immune Hunter unfurled that strangling creeper from her wrist. It shot out like a whip, wrapped itself round Toni’s ankles and dragged her back. Then it flipped her into the sundew. She sank into the monstrous plant, its gluey tentacles reacting to her struggles by closing around her skinny limbs. It drew her in, like a sea anemone does a fish. Jay could hear her stifled, terrified cries.

For a heart-stopping second, Jay thought they were going to leave her there, for the plant to digest. But an Immune Hunter snatched her out, trembling and dripping sticky strands.

'Is she an Immune?' Viridian asked Jay, glowering down at him.

Jay clamped his lips together.

'Well, we'll soon find out,' said Viridian. The Immune Hunters marched Toni away. She looked frail and helpless, with those monstrous mutants towering over her. She threw one desperate, defeated glance back at Jay, then she was gone.

Jay was left alone with Viridian.

Suddenly, the Cultivar released his grip. Jay stared up into Viridian's face. His rage seemed to have disappeared. He even seemed slightly amused, as if he was laughing at some private joke.

Jay, trying to stop his voice from shaking, asked, 'Where's my dad?'

Viridian said softly, 'You didn't think he was here, did you?'

Of course. It had been a trap. And he and Toni had walked straight into it.

Viridian lifted him up by the scruff of his neck.

'Ow!' shouted Jay, as his face brushed the cruel prickles that protected the Supreme Commander's chlorophyll skin and stung like a swarm of angry wasps.

Then Viridian dropped Jay into a carnivorous plant.

For a few mystified seconds, Jay didn't know what had happened. It was like he'd been thrown down a well.

He was in the swollen base of a purple tube. Above him the tube narrowed, its fleshy veined walls rising to a circle of moonlight high above them. Then the light disappeared as the lid to the tube snapped shut to seal him in.

Jay was trapped in a giant pitcher plant.

'Let me out!' he yelled, thumping the walls. They were semi-transparent: he could see blurry shapes outside. But they were really tough. His fists just bounced off them.

'Let me out!' he screamed again. But there was no sound at all from out in the dome.

Panicking, he tried to scale the sides of his prison, but the walls were slippery and smooth, so prey couldn't escape.

Jay slumped down at the bottom of the tube. He was sitting in something wet, the remains of the pitcher plant's last meal. He put his hand down, touched something slimy that felt like a small bone.

'*Yurgh.*' He snatched his hand back out of the stinking soup.

More liquid was rising. He stood up, desperately punching the walls, kicking them. He knew what was happening. Toni had told him. The pitcher was filling with water.

The plant was trying to drown him. When he stopped struggling, its digestive juices would flow from the pitcher walls and dissolve his body, absorbing his nutrients into itself.

Top plant predators. Awesome killing machines. Jay moaned in terror as the liquid crept up to his chest. Toni had said no prey ever escaped. Except wasps, who sawed through the walls with their slicing jaws.

For one frenzied moment, Jay tried to bite his way through, but his teeth just slid off. There was nowhere to get a grip.

Then he remembered Dad's shears. He plunged his arm down in the sticky liquid, found his pocket, felt around. Had he lost them when he fell off the fence?

Sobbing with relief, he found them. The water was up to his armpits now. He stabbed a blade into the pitcher's walls. It went through. Jay tore the shears through the wall, cutting a great zigzag circle.

He dropped the shears and stuck his head out, then plunged the rest of his body through in a gush of water. For minutes he lay curled up on the ground like a soggy newborn kitten. Then his brain started to function again.

Get out of here! it told him.

He hadn't even looked around yet. Maybe Viridian had stayed to watch. Jay raised his head, hardly daring to breathe. But the dome was silent, the carnivorous plants grotesque dark shapes in the moonlight.

Jay dragged himself to the concrete drain. He was sopping wet. His muscles felt so feeble and weak that he could scarcely pull himself through. But then he was out of the dome and staggering for the shelter of the trees.

CHAPTER 16

Afterwards Jay was never sure how he climbed that fence and got back to the science block at Franklin High. But twenty minutes later he was collapsed against the basement door, weak and dizzy, trembling fingers trying to key in the code to the Immune's hideout.

He didn't bother with the sleeping Immunes, but burst into the little room where Dr Moran was working. Dr Moran looked up from his microscope. There was a row of blood-filled test tubes in a rack beside him.

Wild-eyed, sopping wet, near hysterical, Jay gasped, 'Toni... Research Station... Immune Hunters, they've got her.'

Dr Moran grasped Jay by both shoulders, stared into his eyes. 'Take some deep breaths. Try to calm down.' Jay dragged air into his burning lungs. 'Now tell me again.'

Jay dropped his gaze. 'Toni and me went to the Research Station to rescue Dad. Viridian was there. Toni got captured. I only just got away...'

Jay's voice trailed into silence and he braced himself for Dr Moran's reaction.

But Dr Moran didn't say anything. Finally Jay dared to look at his face. It seemed quite calm.

Jay, his nerves already shredded, exploded into anger. 'What's wrong with you?' he yelled. 'Didn't you hear what I said? Toni got caught! You know what they do to Immunes!'

'Toni isn't Immune,' said Dr Moran.

'What?'

'She isn't Immune.'

Jay would have collapsed on the floor if Dr Moran hadn't held him up. 'Sit down,' said Dr Moran, leading him to a chair. 'Before you fall down.'

Jay couldn't believe what he'd just heard. 'Why did you tell Toni she was Immune if she's not?'

Dr Moran sat down at his lab bench. He pushed his microscope aside.

'I suppose I owe you some sort of explanation,' he said. 'Although I'm not sure why, when you got my daughter captured.'

'I didn't make her,' muttered Jay. 'She offered to go.'

Dr Moran gave a weary smile, drew a hand across his forehead. 'Sounds like my Toni,' he said. 'I don't suppose she told you about her mother?'

Jay nodded. 'She told me her mother was – ' And then it crashed into his brain that he had never told Toni that Teal was dead, and that Dr Moran wouldn't know either.

Quickly, he started again. 'Toni told me her mum is a top Cultivar, called Teal.'

Dr Moran nodded. 'I didn't want Toni to follow her mum,' he said. 'I wanted her to be human so she would stay with me.'

'So you told Toni she was Immune?' said Jay.

Dr Moran nodded. 'I knew she wanted to be Verdan. She'd have taken the virus shot.'

'That's why you were worried that she'd been scratched. And that's why you never allowed her out,' said Jay. 'Not because she might get killed, but because she might become Verdan.'

'Perhaps you think that was selfish,' said Dr Moran. 'But I was just doing what I thought was best for Toni.'

What was best for you, you mean, thought Jay. But he didn't want Toni to go Verdan either.

'We've got to go and get her out,' he said. He was sure that, this time, Dr Moran would agree to a rescue.

So he was astonished and horrified when, once again, that steely look came into Dr Moran's eyes and he said, 'No.'

Jay leapt up. 'I can't believe you!'

Dr Moran said, 'Don't you think I want to? But I can't risk my work. I'm so close to a cure – '

'But we're talking about your own daughter!' Jay interrupted.

Dr Moran said, 'Stop shouting. Try to think logically. The scientists at the Research Station have bred super-warriors. We don't stand a chance against them. The Cultivars won't kill Toni, because she's not Immune.'

'How will they find that out?' demanded Jay, and then realised he knew the answer.

'By injecting her with the plant virus, of course,' said Dr Moran. 'So the best thing I can do is find that cure.'

'But once she's Verdan,' said Jay, 'they might punish her with Etiolation.'

Dr Moran obviously hadn't thought of that.

'It's a horrible death,' Jay said urgently. 'They put them in the dark, in a cave. I saw Teal die down there, with fungus all over her and – '

He clamped a hand over his mouth. There was total silence in the room. Then Dr Moran said, 'Did you say you saw Toni's mum die?'

Jay nodded.

'Does Toni know?'

'No,' said Jay. 'I didn't tell her. I didn't know how to.'

Dr Moran got up from the bench. Jay flinched. He actually thought that Dr Moran might attack him. But Dr Moran didn't look at Jay at all, or seem aware of him. He just turned round, without saying a word, and disappeared through a door in a far corner of the room.

Jay sat staring at the door for a few seconds, waiting for Dr Moran to come back. Then he realized, *He isn't going to.*

Jay jumped out of his seat, went over and rattled the door handle. It was locked. He hammered at the door, then kicked at it. It stayed shut.

'You can't just walk away!' he yelled furiously. 'You've got to come back and *do* something!'

Jay thought, *What am I going to do now?* He couldn't stay in this basement. It just seemed like another prison.

He walked, sick and dizzy, through the lab where the Immunes were sleeping. The noise had woken them up. Some were asking blearily, 'What's going on?'

Jay ignored them. He walked out of the basement, into the cool, fresh air and the starry night. He crossed the Franklin High playing fields, stumbling past the group of dormant Verdans, head now so painful he could hardly see, and forced his aching body on towards the motorway and the mine. It was the only refuge he could think of. He could rest there. Think how to rescue Toni and Dad. Then he realised he didn't even know where Dad was being held.

Suddenly he felt horribly weak and ill, as if, any second, he was going to pass out...

CHAPTER 17

Jay was aware for a long time that there was a blurry human face hovering above him. Every time he woke, there it was. He drifted back into sleep, and woke, and there it was again. But now the features were suddenly sharp, in focus.

'Dad!' said Jay, struggling to sit up. 'Is it really you?'

A hand pushed him down again.

'Course it's me,' Dad said. 'Rest. Don't try to talk.'

Jay gazed around him. He was in the back of their old battered van, wrapped in sleeping bags. Candles cast a cosy, yellow glow over the inside. Jay smiled, still only half conscious. Dad was here.

He felt safe, protected, like a little kid tucked up under his duvet, after he'd been read a bedtime story. Everything was fine. Dad was here.

Jay relaxed and just let himself drift away into sleep again.

When Jay woke next, much later, he was more alert. He lay still in his cocoon of sleeping bags, piecing together what had happened.

He had got sick. That was it. He had set off for the mine on foot, and as he had walked, he had felt worse and worse. The dog bite on his hand had throbbed. Everywhere the pitcher plant had touched felt sore and hot. Soon he could barely think. He'd kept staggering along somehow. Finally he must have passed out.

Then Dad must have found him.

Wait a minute! thought Jay. *How did Dad find me? They took him prisoner!*

For a few panicky seconds Jay thought he'd just imagined Dad. That it had all been some feverish hallucination. He sat bolt upright.

'Dad!' he screamed.

Dad climbed into the van and crouched by Jay in the flickering candle light.

'Hey,' he said. 'You look much better. You look almost human.'

'You don't,' said Jay. Dad looked like a wild man. He had a long, straggly beard like Robinson Crusoe.

'Want a drink?' said Dad.

Jay sat up, without feeling too dizzy.

'I was scared for a while there,' said Dad. 'You were really sick. But you're as tough as me. You shook it off, whatever it was.'

Jay sipped the water. He almost wished he was still out of it, floating somewhere in limbo. Because now he'd recovered, all his fears and worries came crowding back.

'How did I get here? Am I back in the mine?'

Dad nodded.

'How did *you* get here?' asked Jay.

'I escaped in the confusion at the rally,' Dad said. 'After they dragged me off the balcony I could hear all kinds of mayhem going on in the square.'

'That was the Immune Hunters,' said Jay, 'after me.'

'Viridian sent his full squad out there, so I was left with this one weedy Cultivar guarding me.' Dad shrugged, but couldn't keep the hint of pride out of his voice, as he went on, 'So I overpowered him. As for you, I found you in the scrubland, passed out. I think you'd tried to walk here. You had a fever. I carried you down to the mine, and I've been looking after you ever since. You had me pretty worried, son.'

'How long have I been here?' asked Jay.

'I don't know,' said Dad. 'You lose track of time down here. About ten days?'

'Ten days!' said Jay, appalled. 'We've got to go right now. We've got to go and find Toni. She could be still at the Research Station. She might be in the Etiolation Cave.'

'The what cave?' said Dad. 'And who's this Toni?'

'She's a girl I met,' said Jay. 'She saved my life.'

* * *

Gradually, in between spooning canned peaches into his mouth, Jay told Dad everything. About the Etiolation Cave and the other Immunes and Dr Moran. About the carnivorous plants and Toni getting caught.

Dad gave a low whistle when Jay had finished. But all he said was, 'You've been a busy boy.'

Jay said, 'I went to the Research Station straight after the rally. I thought they'd bring you back there in the Humvees.'

Dad shook his head. 'I don't think they ever meant to take me there. They planned to infect me with the virus. If I was Immune, they were going to finish me off right away. If I turned Verdan they were talking about punishing me for aiding and abetting an Immune. Probably by chaining me up in that Etiolation Cave.'

'So *are* you Immune then?' asked Jay.

'Don't know,' said Dad. 'They never got the chance to try and infect me. Was your gran all right? Where'd she go, after you got out of the cave?'

Jay said, 'I don't know. She just wandered off, you know, doing what Verdans do. I said I'd go back for her. But...' Jay frowned, shook his head. 'What's the point? She's Verdan now. She doesn't care about us.'

'Yeah, that's Verdans for you. Hey,' said Dad, 'that green freak's freakier than ever, isn't he? I think he fancies himself as some kind of god. I couldn't believe it, you coming right up and asking him to let me go.' Dad shook his head in amazement. 'You're a crazy, hot-headed kid,' he told Jay.

'You remind me of me when I was your age. Want a can of sardines? That's all we've got left to eat.'

'I hate sardines,' said Jay.

But Dad had already leapt out the van. Jay sat there, turning Dad's words, *You remind me of me when I was your age*, round and round in his mind, watching them sparkle, like they were a precious diamond.

It seemed ages before Dad came back with the sardines. Jay said, 'We have to go and get Toni. Her dad won't. He says the only way to help her now is to find a cure for the virus.'

'Maybe he's right,' said Dad.

'What? You mean, we should just *leave* her there?' Jay put a wobbly hand to his head. Getting mad was a bad idea; it had made him dizzy again.

Dad said, 'Look, calm down.' He thrust the can of sardines at Jay. 'Eat those, get your strength back. They're good for you.'

Jay pushed them away. 'I don't want any.'

'You think a lot of this girl, Toni, don't you?'

'Yeah, I do. I really like her.'

'Well, she won't care about *you* any more,' said Dad, bluntly. 'Now she's Verdan.'

'We don't know if they made her go Verdan.'

'Come on,' said Dad. 'Don't kid yourself. Do you really think she'd have any choice?'

Jay's brain, still sore from the illness, felt tied up in knots.

He stared at Dad helplessly. 'I don't know what to do.'

'OK,' said Dad. 'I'm going to say something you won't like. I agree with that Dr Moran guy. I think the best thing we can do is join those Immunes, find a cure for your girlfriend.'

'She's not my girlfriend!'

'Whatever. Where did you say these Immunes are hiding?'

'Franklin High,' said Jay. 'In the science block.'

'Right,' said Dad. 'We need to get out of this mine anyway. Sooner or later those Immune Hunters will come here.'

'But – ' protested Jay.

'We'll go to Franklin High first. Maybe this Dr Moran has already found a cure. You said he was close, didn't you?

'No,' said Jay, 'first we'll go to the Etiolation Cave, see if they've put her in there.' Jay didn't even want to think about the horrors of that – Toni, in the same cave where her mum had died. 'Come on.'

He started struggling out of the sleeping bag, then paused. Even in his frantic impatience, he'd just thought of something. 'I suppose we'd better wait until night time.' The dark didn't seem to affect the Cultivars much. But at least the Verdans would be dormant.

'It is night time out there,' said Dad. 'I just went and checked. So let's go.'

Dad knew the short cut to the cave entrance, across the scrubland, through those weird conical hills.

The night sky was wonderful, a vast, navy blue bowl upturned over Franklin, fizzing with shooting stars. But Jay didn't notice the display. With every step, his dread was growing. 'Dad,' he said, finally. 'When we get to the cave, will you go down there? I don't think...'

'Yeah, course,' said Dad, as if it was no big deal. 'I brought a torch in my backpack.'

'Thanks,' said Jay, gratefully.

The trapdoor was wide open, just the way Jay had left it, days before. Jay stared at it in surprise. Surely, if they'd put someone new in, even if they didn't bother to lock it, the Cultivars would have closed it?

'Stay here,' said Dad, getting his torch out his backpack.

'She's got brown hair,' said Jay. 'It's short where I cut it off. And brown eyes.'

But Dad was already gone, climbing down the limestone blocks into the dark. Jay told himself, *Idiot. She won't look like that now, will she? Not if she's Verdan.*

He waited at the top, his arms hugging his body, trying to calm himself down.

If Toni was down there, would she be still alive? How long had Teal lasted in that terrible prison? If Toni was still alive, would she come back with them? Or would she just slide away into the greenery like Gran? What would they do then?

Jay stared round at the derelict industrial estate. Some units were collapsing, invaded by strangling ivy and thorny bramble creepers. Jay half-expected to see Gran, crouched in some weeds, conserving energy until daylight came.

'Hey.'

Jay nearly jumped out of his skin. It was Dad, just behind him. 'Was she down there?'

'No-one's down there. I checked everywhere. The cave is empty. Apart from that Cultivar you told me about.'

'Is she dead?' asked Jay.

'Oh yes,' said Dad, grim-faced. 'She's dead, all right.' He put his torch away in his backpack. 'Right. Let's go and find this Moran guy.'

'You won't like him,' warned Jay.

'Doesn't matter,' said Dad. 'If he's found a cure for this virus, he's a hero.'

CHAPTER 18

As they walked through the abandoned housing estate to get to Franklin High, they saw Verdans, hundreds of them, creeping out of the undergrowth.

'They don't usually move around at night,' said Jay. 'Where are they all going?'

Dad said, 'They're not even looking at us.'

He walked right out into the street to prove it. The Verdans' green eyes didn't even flicker in his direction. They just flowed around him, staring ahead, all going the same way, trudging slowly.

'Maybe Viridian's having another rally in the square,' Jay suggested.

'At midnight?'

The Verdans were a sad, sickly bunch, creeping along like refugees in their own town. Their clothes were ragged, their chlorophyll skin scaly and withered brown in places. Some had even caught plant infestations: red spider mites running through their hair, greenfly clinging to their eyebrows and eyelashes, circles of orange rust mould on their skin. One had a slug latched onto his neck. It had crawled up his arm, leaving a silvery trail.

'Where are the Cultivars?' said Jay.

Cultivars would be easily spotted. They'd stand out a mile in this shuffling crowd, with their superior strength and extra height, their dark green skin glowing with health and vigour, their eyes blazing with ruthless fanaticism. But there weren't any.

More and more Verdans swelled the throng. It seemed like the whole population of Franklin was lurching along zombie-like in the moonlight towards the same destination, with Jay and Dad tagging along behind.

'Look!' whispered Jay to Dad. Ahead were some Verdans with yellow skin. Some were ghostly pale, almost transparent, like wraiths.

'Those must be the prisoners, from the cave.'

The prisoners dragged themselves along painfully slowly. The feeblest were crawling like spiders on long, etiolated limbs. Yet they all seemed intent on getting somewhere.

'I don't understand it,' said Jay, baffled. 'Before, they were so scared of Cultivars, they wouldn't leave even though the trapdoor was wide open. So how come they're going now?'

Jay plunged in among the etiolated Verdans. 'Have you seen a girl called Toni?' he asked them. He grabbed one jelly-like yellow arm. 'Was she down in the cave with you?'

But they just gazed at him with their spooky, pale eyes and plodded on.

At the end of the estate, the Verdans turned right, towards Franklin High and the Research Station.

'They're going our way,' said Jay. 'You don't reckon they know where Dr Moran and the Immunes are?'

But the Verdans didn't turn off at Franklin High.

'Look,' said Jay, 'there's loads more of them, around the Research Station.'

Dad glanced at Jay. 'Shall we see what's going on?'

'Yes,' said Jay, eagerly. 'Toni must be in there.'

'She might be,' said Dad. 'Look Jay, don't get too excited. Even if we find her, she might not be alive.'

But Jay wasn't listening. He'd already dashed off. Dad raced after him.

The Verdans flowed through the lifted Security Barrier like a surging green tide. They surrounded the domes, pressing up against the glass walls.

Maybe they've come to overthrow Viridian, thought Jay, excitedly.

But when he looked at them, he could see how stupid that was. This wasn't a mass uprising. The Verdans weren't co-operating with each other, or even communicating. They just milled silently about. Why had they come here? What were they waiting for?

Then Jay realized.

They were waiting for someone to come out of the domes and tell them what to do.

But no-one came. Not Viridian, or an Immune Hunter, or

even a Cultivar. The Verdans parted as Jay pushed his way to the front, peered into the dome.

The glass was covered on the inside with black slime.

Suddenly, he heard Dad shouting, 'Jay, where are you?'

Jay dived through the Verdans again, until he found Dad, who clutched his arm. Jay had never seen him so excited.

'Dr Moran's here,' said Dad. 'He's found a cure! He's giving it to the Verdans now. The Cultivars will be out any second to stop him. We have to help.'

'Something's happened inside the dome, Dad,' said Jay. But Dad was already striding away.

'Come on,' he yelled back to Jay. 'Dr Moran needs all the help he can get.'

On the edge of the crowd, they found Dr Moran and the other Immunes. They were frantically giving the Verdans the vaccine, squirting it into their mouths from little plastic bottles. The Verdans were so used to obeying orders that they simply opened their mouths wide like baby birds.

Dad said, 'Here, give me some of that stuff, I'll help.'

'Six drops each,' said Dr Moran, his face haggard and grey with fatigue.

Jay sidled up close to Dr Moran – he didn't want Dad to hear their conversation. 'Give me one of those bottles.'

'What do you want it for?' Dr Moran asked Jay. 'Are you going to help?'

'I'm going to take it into the dome,' said Jay, 'and if I find Toni, I'm going to give her the vaccine.'

Dr Moran's haughty face suddenly crumpled. His lip trembled.

'Thank you,' was all he said, handing Jay a bottle of vaccine. 'Make sure she gets six drops.' Then he carried on with his work, saving the human species.

Jay raced up to Dad, who'd been barging through the crowd, dosing every Verdan that got in his way. Now some of them were clamouring for the vaccine. 'Stand in line!' Dad was telling them. 'You'll get your turn.'

Jay dodged between Verdans, unzipped Dad's backpack, got out the torch. Then he raced, with the torch and the precious bottle of vaccine, to the second dome. Like the first dome, he couldn't see inside; its glass walls were coated, on the inside, with sticky black stuff. He found a door but it was locked. The drain was the one sure way he knew to get in. He hardly noticed that the bright green algae that lined it had turned black. He just wriggled through, to the other side.

CHAPTER 19

Jay played the torch beam around and gave a sharp intake of breath.

It was like a plant morgue in here. The giant pitcher plants, sundews and Venus fly traps were all dead or dying. Some were covered in black sooty mould, some had already collapsed into black slimy jelly. There was a terrible stink of rotting vegetation. Jay took a step and a cloud of buzzing bluebottles rose up from the decayed remains of some plant.

Jay walked through the slimy graveyard. Great sheets of black slime hung from plants, like funeral flags. Strings of sticky gloop stuck to his soles of his shoes.

'What's happened?' Jay murmured, horrified. Then he saw a pitcher plant leaf, not as putrefied as the others. It was covered in fuzzy black dots that seemed very familiar.

Black spot fungus, thought Jay. The disease Toni's carnivorous plants had. The most deadly plant fungus there was.

Maybe he and Toni had brought it here, on their hands and clothes. Toni had said it was very contagious. The dome, with its extra light and heat, had provided the perfect conditions for its spores to grow and spread like smallpox in humans.

It felt like a small triumph, destroying Viridian's collection of killing machines. As if, at last, humans had started to fight back.

Jay headed into the third dome to search for Toni. She'd said the Cultivars' living quarters were there, and the labs, where the Verdan scientists did their experiments. She'd said that was the most likely place they'd keep a prisoner.

A sliding door between the domes stood open. His torch beam lit up a wide, empty corridor, with doors on either side. He played his torch around some more, looking for signs of life.

But the only thing he saw was the fungus. It had spread even here, creeping like a sinister black tide up the walls.

He stepped into the corridor, crept along it. He switched off his torch, since dim yellow lights were glowing from the corridor's ceiling. He came to a T-junction. Which way now? He gazed down the left-hand corridor, then the right.

Was there something moving, at the end of the right-hand corridor? His eyes strained through the gloom, trying to see. Then the shadows suddenly took form.

There was a mob of Cultivars at the other end, racing this way, sprinting on long, green springy legs. There was no way he could outrun them. Jay held his hands up in surrender.

At the last second he realized, *They aren't going to stop!*

He flung himself against a wall so he didn't get trampled. Dozens streamed past. The last one grabbed his throat. It was the woman Immune Hunter and Jay thought he was done for. But she didn't use her strangling tendrils. And Jay saw that her green skin was spotted with black mould.

She thrust her diseased face into his, showing her teeth in a green snarl. 'I need the vaccine. Have you got it?'

Jay's hand was clasped round the vaccine for Toni, in his pocket. There was no way he was going to give that up.

Jay stammered, half-choking, 'Dr Moran's got it, outside.'

She flung him back against the wall and sprinted away.

Jay staggered away from the wall, coughing. He turned down the right-hand corridor. The fungus was here too, sliming the walls. It had spread right into the heart of the Cultivar HQ.

The corridor opened into a larger space, dimly lit. There were benches, with big, powerful lamps positioned over them. None of the lamps was switched on. Fungus dripped from them, like Gothic Christmas decorations.

Jay slipped on the slimy floor, and almost fell into a black rotting heap by one of the benches.

He sprang back, swallowed the sour bile rising in his throat. The heap was all that remained of a Cultivar.

Fighting nausea, Jay peered closer. It was the Immune Hunter, the one who'd crouched, waiting, underwater, when he and Toni had gone to the shipping container. Jay could tell by the sticky hairs, black now, on one outstretched hand.

The fungus had killed him.

Now he noticed there were blackened heaps here and there around the room. Other Immune Hunters?

Jay didn't wait to find out. He yelled, 'Toni? Are you here?'

Unbearable thoughts tormented him. If they'd made Toni Verdan, maybe she'd caught this fungus too.

He yelled again, 'Toni, where are you?'

Then, from somewhere in the room, came a groan. Someone was still alive.

Jay saw something twitching by the door. He raced over. But it wasn't Toni.

It was Viridian.

The Cultivar Commander's massive body lay stretched out on the floor. Black mould covered his skin. He raised his crested head like a sick dinosaur. The fire in his eyes wasn't as bright as before but it was still burning.

Jay crouched down beside him. He said, 'Where's Toni?'

'It was the grafts,' said Viridian. Black spores puffed out as he spoke.

'I asked you about Toni!'

'We used our carnivorous plants for grafts,' said Viridian, coughing out spores like smoke. 'The fungus spread through our bodies. We infected the other Cultivars. Then our best warriors started dying...'

He moved his great head from side to side. He almost seemed to be smiling in admiration, that such a powerful elite had been brought down by a humble fungus.

Black tears rolled down his face. He said, 'I wanted to go further. Much further. But it's too late for me...' His voice trailed away.

Jay shook him angrily. 'Don't you die yet!'

Viridian had opened his eyes. He was smiling. 'This has been the biggest adventure ever.' He grasped Jay's arm with one mouldy hand, as if they were friends. '*The biggest adventure ever.*'

Then Jay saw how Viridian had got the fungus. The Commander had a graft, surgically implanted into his wrist. It was a beautiful little Venus fly trap, too small to be a weapon. Had he had it put there like some kind of living jewellery? To feed it like a pet?

Jay shuddered. He couldn't believe that once he'd thought they had something in common.

'Where's Toni,' said Jay again. 'Tell me!'

A new fire flamed deep in Viridian's eyes. 'Toni,' he repeated. 'She is our legacy. Our greatest creation. She is the Future.'

'Where is she?' Jay shouted. 'What have you done to her?' He reached out to shake the dying Commander's shoulder, but then snatched back his hand as he remembered those stinging spines that bristled all over his chest and shoulders.

'Toni's an angel now,' said Viridian.

'You killed her!' yelled Jay.

'I can die happy,' said Viridian, 'knowing she's an angel.'

Then, with a smile on his face, Viridian turned his head aside and closed his eyes.

'I hope you're dead, you sadistic freak!' screamed Jay.

He sprang up from Viridian's body and hardly knowing where he was going, raced out of the terrible room. He ran wildly, almost crashing into a wall. Instead of backing off he started hitting it, over and over again, howling out his grief for Toni. He stopped when he saw his knuckles were bleeding.

He wiped snot and tears from his face and walked on, very upright, eyes straight ahead.

He was in a corridor with a glass wall. On the other side of the glass was a science lab. Or was it an operating theatre? It didn't seem important any more.

He shouldered his way through another set of doors, carefully keeping his mind numb, and saw he was in a little triangular outdoor courtyard between the three domes. Overhead the stars still sparkled, the moon still looked down.

There were three or four trees, bunched together in the courtyard. Jay heard a rustle behind them. Could it be an Immune Hunter, who'd somehow escaped the fungus infestation? Jay tried to make himself care. He looked wearily towards the trees.

An angel rose above the courtyard trees and hovered there, beating its great wings. Except it wasn't a heavenly angel. It had green skin. And the wings on its back weren't feathery white, but green, edged with spines like teeth and deep blood-red inside. They'd been grafted on from a giant Venus fly trap.

The Research Station's scientists had performed the surgery. They'd called their latest creation *Venus Angel*.

The Venus Angel slowly flapped its beautiful, deadly wings. It gazed down at Jay. Its green eyes seemed totally alien – there was nothing human in them at all. Its green hair was spiky, hacked off.

'Toni!' gasped Jay

They'd made her Verdan. They'd put wings onto her back. But she was alive. A rush of joy took Jay's breath away. He scrabbled in his hoodie pocket for the vaccine bottle. He couldn't find it. Feverishly, he searched again. It was definitely gone. He'd dropped it somewhere, in his frantic rush through the dome.

The magnificent, mutant creature came closer. She swooped down from the tree tops until she was right in front of Jay. She snapped her main wings shut. Smaller Venus fly trap wings on her wrists and ankles were beating fast like hummingbird wings, keeping her centimetres above the ground.

Now her eyes were on a level with Jay's. She looked at him curiously, but totally without fear. Like you'd look at some weird caterpillar that had suddenly wriggled across your path.

'Toni?' said Jay. He thought he saw a gleam of recognition suddenly flash across her face. 'Toni, it's me, Jay.'

The Angel said, 'Jay?' They stared at each other without speaking. She opened her mouth to say something more.

A door crashed behind Jay. Dr Moran came racing out into the courtyard. He stopped for a moment, astonished, as he recognised his daughter.

Then he came running up. 'Toni!' he cried. 'It's all right. I've found a cure. We can make you human again. We can take those horrible things off your back...'

He held out a bottle of vaccine. 'Just open your mouth. And this nightmare will all be over.'

Toni raised an arm, her wrist wings vibrating in a crimson-green blur. Contemptuously, she dashed the bottle out of his hand. It went rolling away across the courtyard.

'Toni!' yelled Dr Moran. He went racing after the bottle. Toni opened her main wings. With one last look at Jay, she rose into the air.

'Wait!' shouted Dr Moran.

But a Venus Angel doesn't obey human commands. In all her terrible splendour, Toni rose above the domes.

'I'll come and find you!' yelled Jay. 'I promise!'

He had no idea whether she heard or not. For seconds Toni hovered, the moonlight shining through her wings. Then she soared higher into the night sky until she was lost among the stars.

CHAPTER 20

Dr Moran and Jay walked back through the domes in silence.

Dr Moran spoke first. 'I'll find her,' he said. 'It's not too late to make her human again.'

'*I'll* find her,' Jay said.

He felt clear-headed and full of purpose. He didn't know yet *how* he was going to find Toni. But he knew he would never give up until he did.

Then a terrible thought struck him, 'What if she's infected with the black spot fungus?' he asked.

'She isn't,' replied the doctor with certainty.

'How can you be so sure?' Jay demanded. 'She got grafted, and Viridian said the fungus spread through grafts. Viridian's dying,' he added. 'He's probably dead by now.'

Dr Moran looked at Jay, astonished. 'Are you sure?'

'I've just seen him,' said Jay. But he wasn't interested in Viridian any more. All he cared about was Toni.

He challenged Dr Moran again. 'How'd you know Toni's not infected?'

'Once the Cultivar scientists found out about the black spot, they made their labs sterile, used plants that were fungus free. They kept Toni in quarantine after surgery. So she never caught it.'

'Who told you all this?' Jay asked him.

'That Immune Hunter who ran out of the dome. I refused to give her the vaccine until she did. She was one of my colleagues once,' added Dr Moran. 'A very good scientist.'

They were passing the labs behind the glass walls. 'See?' said Dr Moran.

'See what?' said Jay, his eyes sweeping over the gleaming stainless steel surfaces, the white walls. Then he caught on. 'There's no fungus in there.'

Dr Moran nodded. 'That's why I think there's still hope for Toni. If I can find her.'

'*I'll* find her,' said Jay again. Nothing on earth was going to stop him.

'So where's Viridian?' asked Dr Moran. 'I've never seen him. I'd like to take a look at him.'

'He's in here,' said Jay, steeling himself, as they entered the black, stinking room full of slimy heaps that had once been Immune Hunters. 'Over there.' Jay pointed. He couldn't bear to look. 'He doesn't look anything like he did before,' he added.

No one seeing Viridian now could imagine him as he'd been at the rally burning, like a fiery green comet, with such fierce and brilliant energy. On that balcony he'd seemed indestructible. Franklin was far too small for all that power. You just knew he wouldn't stop until he ruled the planet.

Dr Moran said, 'There's nothing here. He's gone.'

'He can't have,' said Jay. 'He was dead when I left him. Or nearly.'

'Come and look.'

Reluctantly, Jay went over. Viridian's body was gone, only a sooty spoor print on the ground to show where it had been.

'Look,' said Dr Moran, grim-faced. There were smudgy hand prints, knee prints dragging across the floor.

'He can't be still alive,' whispered Jay. 'I mean, he was eaten away by fungus, he was breathing out spores.'

'In that case, he's finished,' said Dr Moran. 'He's crawled away to die somewhere.'

'Yeah,' agreed Jay, reassured. 'Yeah. That's what must have happened.'

* * *

It was dawn when Toni, scanning the ground from the sky, found a suitable place to land. It was a swampy wilderness, perfect for carnivorous plants. She was exhausted and starving. A black-backed gull flew too close. It hardly had time to squawk before Toni's main wings snapped shut on it.

She drifted down to the swamp but landed clumsily: she still had a great deal to learn about flying.

Toni crouched on the boggy ground, on bright green cushions of moss. In each direction stretched fields of ghostly white pitcher plants, a metre high. Tiny sundew plants glistened in between them like rubies, with gnats struggling in their sticky tentacles.

A picture came into her mind. It was of a human boy called Jay shouting, 'I'll come and find you!' and getting smaller and smaller as she soared away into the sky. The image disturbed her, she didn't know why. She felt a stab of intense loneliness and longing. The pain was so sharp, it made her clutch at her heart. But then it passed and she forgot it.

An hour later, Toni had finished digesting the soft tissue of the seagull. She let the bones, beak, feet and feathers fall out of her gorgeous wings and stared around, surveying her new kingdom.

THE STORY CONTINUES

Coming in October 2013

VIRIDIAN: VENUS ANGEL

Read on...

VIRIDIAN: VENUS ANGEL

Toni was in the swamplands, south of Franklin. Since she'd flown away from Jay and Dr Moran, she hadn't seen a single human. No-one, not even Verdans, came to these quaking bogs, where carnivorous plants thrived. But, to a Venus Angel, it felt like coming home.

Toni crouched among pitcher plants, rising around her, a metre high. From inside their traps, tall slender trumpets, she could hear the frantic whine of flies. They'd crawled in and couldn't climb back up the slippery walls. Now they were being digested, slowly.

All the predator plants had caught something. Tiny sundews had gnats struggling in their sticky tentacles. Venus fly traps had their leaves clamped shut, like clam shells. Inside them insects were being slowly drained of body fluids.

Toni watched them fondly, as if they were subjects in her own personal kingdom.

'Good hunting,' she told them, smiling.

She still used English to think and talk to herself, sometimes. But her human speech was getting rusty. It belonged to that other world she'd lived in before she became a Venus Angel and had to learn a whole new set of skills to survive.

She still thought about that boy sometimes. What was his name?

'Jay,' Toni said out loud. Her voice seemed strange, as if it belonged to someone else. She said 'Jay,' again, to reassure herself that the sound was coming out of her own mouth.

In her mind, she suddenly saw him, far below her, heard his frantic cry: 'I'll come and find you. I promise!'

Then a screech came from above her. Toni looked up. She forgot about Jay. A hawk came streaking in from the west. Bam! It hit a pigeon in the air above her. There was an explosion of feathers and the hawk spiralled off, the pigeon grasped in its talons. Its harsh wild cries faded into the distance.

Toni's green lips curved into a grin. She'd learned a lot from hawks.

'You were useless at flying before,' she told herself.

But now she was getting better. Better at flying and hunting. Like the hawk, she snatched birds to eat out of the air now, sometimes squirrels from trees. Her wings snapped shut in a tenth of a second.

She opened her glossy, green wings. Bones and grey fur fell out in a neat, dry package. Her wings were blood red inside, rich with nutrients from the squirrel she'd just finished digesting. She took all her meals through her wings now. She'd stopped eating by mouth completely. It was like she'd forgotten how.

She spread her gorgeous wings wide, to soak up the sun. Her green neck twisted, like a plant stem, so her face could bask in its rays. She stayed like that, totally still, for ages, half gargoyle, half beautiful stone angel.

'Time to fly,' Toni told herself.